"Maybe you need to cry more o~~ften~~"

"I feel guilty," she said. "And I know that doesn't make any sense. As an adult, I know it doesn't. But I still feel guilty that I wasn't there to save her. If I'd been there, maybe...maybe..."

Her voice hitched. And that did it.

Ben didn't care that he barely knew her. He didn't care that for the last few weeks he was sure she hated him. And he didn't care that Isabel was probably watching from down the beach with a damn pair of binoculars at this point. He just wanted to hold her.

Stepping forward, he did what he'd wanted to do since that first day he'd seen her outside the candy shop. Breathing hard after chasing Hunter, her cheeks pink, her eyes compassionate despite everything. And he pulled her gently to him.

He didn't say anything. Instead, he wrapped his arms around her and held her close. The wind blew strands of her hair across his face, bringing with it the smell of her shampoo. He hadn't planned this. He'd never meant to touch her at all. But that was the thing about Kyla. Everything about her was turning out to be a surprise.

Dear Reader,

It is with the greatest joy that I introduce to you the first book in my Sisters of Christmas Bay series, *Their Sweet Coastal Reunion*. Although Christmas Bay is a fictional town on the Oregon Coast, it feels like a very real place in my heart. A place where love and family live, and where romance and happily-ever-afters are realized. It's my hope that with Kyla and Ben's story, it's also a place that you'll want to come back to again and again.

So, snuggle up in your coziest chair, have a cup of tea and imagine the sound of waves crashing in the distance. Welcome to Christmas Bay, reader. I'm so glad you're here.

Kaylie Newell

Their Sweet Coastal Reunion

KAYLIE NEWELL

HARLEQUIN

SPECIAL
EDITION

HARLEQUIN®
SPECIAL EDITION™

Recycling programs for this product may not exist in your area.

ISBN-13: 978-1-335-72441-0

Their Sweet Coastal Reunion

Copyright © 2022 by Kaylie Newell

Harlequin Enterprises ULC
22 Adelaide St. West, 41st Floor
Toronto, Ontario M5H 4E3, Canada
www.Harlequin.com

Printed in U.S.A.

For **Kaylie Newell**, storytelling is in the blood. Growing up the daughter of two writers, she knew eventually she'd want to follow in their footsteps. She's now the proud author of over twenty books, including the RITA® finalists *Christmas at the Graff* and *Tanner's Promise*.

Kaylie lives in Southern Oregon with her husband, two daughters, a blind Doberman and two indifferent cats.

Visit Kaylie at Facebook.com/kaylienewell.

Visit the Author Profile page at Harlequin.com.

Most little girls think their dads are the best.
I was lucky. Mine really was.

This one's for you, Dad. I love you.

K.

Chapter One

"How much for the jawbreakers?"

Kyla Beckett smiled at the teenage boy in the faded hoodie and worn-out Converse All Stars. His face looked drawn and a little sad. Something about him reminded her of herself at that age. Except her clothes had never looked as good as his. Her mom had always bought them two sizes too big, so she wouldn't grow out of them so fast.

"Fifty cents each," she said from behind the vintage Formica countertop.

He nodded, his blue eyes shifting toward the tip jar.

He was her first customer of the day. Coastal Sweets was empty this morning. A fine mist was coming down outside, and the Pacific Ocean churned a few blocks away, gray and moody to match the dark, mottled clouds overhead. But Main Street still managed to look cheerful, with colorful flower baskets hanging outside the shop windows, and coffee-clutching tourists beginning to stroll by, unfazed by the weather.

Kyla had almost forgotten this. How charming Christmas Bay could be. After all, the town had coaxed her back into its arms after all these years, something she never thought would happen.

The boy shifted on his feet, suddenly looking nervous.

Kyla's stomach dropped. *Uh-oh.* She was helping Frances with the shop for the summer, but she was also a high school history teacher, and she recognized the look in his eyes. He was getting ready to say something stupid, or do something stupid. And judging by the way he'd just yanked his hood over his head, she was betting on the latter.

But before she could step out from behind the counter, he'd reached out and grabbed the tip jar. Overflowing because Frances had forgotten to empty it last night, and Kyla had unlocked the doors before remembering to do it herself.

"Hey!"

The kid didn't skip a beat. Quick as a cat, he shoved the plastic jar up his hoodie, and bolted for the door.

Kyla didn't hesitate. She hauled herself over the counter and ran after him. Feeling a flash of anger for Frances, who was sweet and loved everyone, and who didn't deserve this. She would've given the kid the money if he'd just asked for it.

"Hey, come back here!"

She winced even as the words left her mouth. Did she actually think he would? But she was out the door and yelling it again before she could help herself.

He glanced back at her, and before she could process the scene playing out before her eyes, he ran right into a uniformed police officer, nearly knocking him off his feet.

The boy fell backward with a grunt and landed on his butt. Hard. The tip jar tumbled out of his hoodie and rolled onto the wet sidewalk. Thankfully the lid stayed on tight.

Kyla slowed, watching as he scrambled to his feet. But he wasn't fast enough to duck around the officer, who grabbed his hoodie and yanked him to a stop.

"Whoa, whoa, whoa. Where do you think you're going?"

The boy didn't struggle. All the life went out of him, and his shoulders slumped. Resigned. Maybe resigned to this world.

In spite of her anger, Kyla's heart squeezed as she made her way toward them. Just like the clothes were familiar, so was that look. Maybe all the fight had gone out of him because there hadn't been that much to begin with.

She wrapped her arms around herself, the mist clinging to her hair and eyelashes. She was glad she'd worn waterproof mascara this morning. She'd been away from the Oregon coast for a while now, but she'd remembered that little necessity.

The officer looked up as she approached. Midthirties. Tall, dark hair, dark eyes. Thick chest and strong biceps that bulged from underneath his uniform sleeves.

He was a good-looking man, no doubt. But that wasn't why Kyla's mouth grew suddenly dry at the sight of him. His body might've changed and matured, but she'd know that face anywhere. His eyes, the set of his mouth, were so familiar, so sweet, that she nearly forgot she hated him.

"I'm guessing he belongs to you?" he said.

Struggling for her bearings, she lifted her chin. *Defensiveness.* She felt it all rushing back. The anger, the pain, the closing off of her heart so nobody could hurt her. How easy it was to step back into those little girl's shoes.

"No. Well, kind of."

He raised his brows.

It was obvious he didn't recognize her. After all, the last time he'd seen her she'd been in the sixth grade, tiny for her age and skinny as a post. Crooked glasses because contacts had never been an option.

Kyla felt the sting of tears at the unwanted memories. She'd worked hard over the years to lock them away. But she also knew that coming back here would open that door again. She just hadn't expected how bright the light would be, or how much it would hurt her eyes.

Gritting her teeth, she pulled the sea air into her lungs. She wouldn't cry out here on this blustery sidewalk in front of the whole town. And she certainly wouldn't cry in front of this man, who, for better or worse, had changed her life forever.

"I'm assuming you'll want to press charges?" he asked.

Kyla thought about this. Christmas Bay was a tourist town, full of little shops like Coastal Sweets. Shoplifters were a problem, and as far as she knew, weren't given much leniency in the hopes of discouraging more shoplifting. It made sense. Still, she couldn't quite bring herself to go there yet.

"How long do I have, Officer?" she asked. Not saying his name, even though his shiny gold name tag practically shouted *Martinez* right there in front of her face. "To decide?"

He frowned, looking down at the boy, whose hoodie was still wadded up in his hand. "Oh. Well, you can take your time. If that's what you want."

Judging by his tone, it was pretty clear he thought she should go ahead and do it. Of course, he would. The Ben Martinez she remembered was a rule follower. He probably wasn't used to bending them much, and quite honestly, neither was she. But she was also having a hard time ignoring the heaviness in her chest at the sight of this kid's threadbare clothes. Of the weariness in his expression. His wavy blond hair hung over one eye, and it wasn't too hard to imagine it in ringlets when he was little.

She watched him, doing her best to lock Ben and his judgment out altogether.

"What's your name?" Kyla asked.

"Hunter."

"How old are you, Hunter?"

"Fifteen."

"You should know that we donate the money in that tip jar to our local food bank at the end of every week. You're old enough to understand how wrong stealing it is. And the implications something like that has on other people."

Hunter had the decency to blush at that. He looked down at his Converses, as Ben let go of his hoodie and smoothed it out.

"I'm sorry," he mumbled.

Kyla relaxed a little. He seemed reasonably contrite, and in her experience, contrition went a long way. That didn't mean he'd quit shoplifting. But maybe he'd think twice next time.

"I know who your dad is," Ben said. "So, I know where you live. I'll be in touch, but until then, no more trouble from you—got it?"

Hunter nodded.

But at the mention of his father, it looked like the weight of the world had just settled squarely on his shoulders.

Kyla took a step back, suddenly overwhelmed with the emotion of it all. With the expression on the boy's face, and the thumping of her heart brought on by the simple presence of the man beside her. She longed for the warmth and comfort of the little candy shop down the street—a place where she could safely unpack the events of the last few minutes.

"I have to get back to the shop now, Officer," she said. "Thank you." She turned and left, hoping he couldn't see the pain in her eyes.

Ben watched the woman walk away, her gray cardigan not doing a ton to conceal her curves. But her curves weren't what had his attention right then. It was her eyes, dove gray, like the sweater. Something about her tickled his memory. He knew her from somewhere, he just couldn't put his finger on it.

"Wait!" he called after her. "Wait just a second…"

She turned, and he jogged to catch up. They were going the same way anyway. The police station was only three doors down from Coastal Sweets.

He smiled as he approached, but her expression remained cool. He couldn't figure out why. Unless maybe he knew her from a police matter or something, but he didn't think so. She had the guarded look of someone who wanted to keep her distance, and that wasn't something he'd be able to let go of easily. Especially not without knowing why.

He stopped a few feet in front of her. Her dark hair was damp now, and starting to curl a little around her collarbone. She hugged the tip jar to her stomach, and gazed up at him, a familiar tilt to her chin.

"So, you're working at the shop?" he asked, trying to sound casual, but feeling anything but. She looked like she wanted to stick a knife between his ribs.

"Yes."

"I didn't know Frances hired someone. I'm glad. She stays pretty busy."

"She does."

He smiled again and stuck out his hand. In his line of work, he found that charm went a long way. In getting people to trust you, in getting them to open up. And he knew for a fact that he had some to spare. Or so he'd been told.

"Ben Martinez. Christmas Bay's police chief."

Her gaze fell to his hand, but she didn't extend hers. She looked back up, her full lips pursed. Okay, now he was getting annoyed. What the hell had he done to her anyway?

"I know who you are," she said.

He dropped his hand to his side. "Well, you're one up on me then, because I've been trying to figure out who you are for the last five minutes."

She shifted on her feet and glanced over at the candy store. "I should go. In case we get a customer."

"Is Frances not working today? I've been meaning to come see her."

He knew he should shut up, but he couldn't help it. He didn't want to leave her just yet.

"She's not," she said. "I talked her into taking the day off."

"Oh, that's great…" He let his voice trail off as they stood there looking at each other. A gull squawked overhead, and a woman brushed by walking a little dog in a sweater. It stopped to sniff Ben's boot and she tugged on its leash. He barely noticed.

"You know," he said. "I gotta say, I'm feeling some hostility coming from you."

She swallowed visibly and looked away, probably not expecting him to call her on it. Another Ben Martinez tactic. Be direct. That one he'd learned from Gracie, who could get anyone talking. Six years old, and already a better negotiator than him.

The woman was quiet, gazing toward the ocean in the distance. The sun was trying its best to peek through the misty clouds overhead and warm things up. It felt good on his shoulders.

"Are you?" he asked.

"Am I what?"

"Hostile. Toward me."

She looked back at him, her lovely eyes chilly. "A little."

He felt his lips tilt at that. She was going to be a challenge, and he liked those.

"Can I ask why?"

"You have no idea who I am?" she asked. "None at all?"

Not yet. But her face was so familiar that it was bringing back feelings, if not clear memories. Feelings from a long time ago. Maybe they'd been friends as kids?

"Not at the moment," he said. "But you're from Christmas Bay, right? Did you go to high school here?"

"I did, but not with you. You were older than me."

She took a breath, and readjusted the tip jar under her arm. "I was friends with Isabel. I lived a few blocks down from you on Poppy Lane…"

Ben's heartbeat slowed inside his chest. Those eyes. He knew those eyes. In fact, right then, he was surprised he could've ever forgotten them.

"I'm Kyla Beckett," she said evenly.

He stood there staring down at her. Taking her in as if she'd slapped him across the face.

She couldn't blame him. She felt the same way. She was still having a hard time reconciling this adult Ben with the boy she'd known before—charismatic, sweet, protective. Protective of her. He'd been her best friend's oldest brother. A star running back, who'd been getting ready to head off to college and a full-ride scholarship. And he'd been her first love, although of course, he never knew that.

He was also the reason she'd finally been taken away from her mother, and placed in Frances's home high above Cape Longing. She'd never gone back. Her mother had died before she ever got the chance.

Ben had been the one to report the neglect, and as far as Kyla was concerned, had betrayed her in the worst way. At least that's how she'd felt as a girl. Now, as a grown woman, she didn't know how she felt. Sad. Angry. Angry that she hadn't had more time with her mother. He couldn't have understood that her mom was a good mom, she just struggled.

Or maybe she was just making excuses again. She was great at those.

"Kyla…" he said quietly.

His deep voice stroked something inside her. A feeling of warmth, of safety. And she pushed it away before it could burrow its way inside her heart. She didn't need anyone's protection anymore. She was fine on her own. Frances had raised her and her foster sisters to be strong, independent women. But it wasn't until right then that Kyla wondered if that independence might've been stoked a little too well. Sometimes, she had flashes of wanting to lean on people again, of needing them in her life. And then the feeling was gone before she could ever get her arms around it.

"It was a long time ago," she said.

He nodded. What could he say? Maybe there wasn't anything *to* say. Maybe from now on, they'd just politely ignore each other around town, pretending like they weren't ever a significant part of each other's lives once.

"How's Isabel?" she asked before she could help it.

He swallowed, his Adam's apple bobbing up and down. Her gaze kept dropping to his mouth, to his jawline, which promised a five-o'clock shadow by noon. He looked handsome in his dark uniform, which was crisp and fitted, even in the mist of the morning.

"She's doing well," he answered. "She's the only

one of my brothers and sisters who still lives here. She's a nurse-practitioner—Frances probably told you that part. Married, kids."

Kyla warmed. She'd genuinely loved Isabel Martinez, and before she'd come to live with Stella and Marley, she was the only sister she'd ever known.

"Tell her I said hello," she said.

"I'll tell her. But don't be surprised if she comes down here as soon as she hears you're back."

Kyla nodded and took a step away, wanting to increase the space between them. Standing this close, she could smell a faint scent of soap, maybe the shampoo he'd used that morning. It was making her a little heady, and she had to remind herself she didn't want anything to do with this man.

He must've noticed the expression on her face, because his softened. But to his credit, he didn't bring up her mother, or the past or anything that could make her chest grow any tighter than it already was.

Instead, he put his hands in his pockets, making his uniform shirt stretch over his broad shoulders. "You should know this isn't the Mohatt boy's first rodeo."

"The Mohatt boy?"

He nodded toward the tip jar. "Our friend who borrowed that. He's a handful."

"Oh. Well, I'm used to those. I'm a teacher."

He eyed her.

"A high school teacher," she continued. "That's

why I can help Frances with the shop. Summer vacation."

"Ahh. So, you're leaving in the fall then. Going back to…"

The truth was, she had nowhere to go. She'd given her notice at her school district in Portland a few weeks ago, packed up her rented cottage and had driven down the coastline not knowing exactly how long she'd be in Christmas Bay. She was here to help with the shop, but Frances was going to need a lot more than that. The big old house on the cape was getting to be too much for her, and her memory was slipping noticeably. Something that worried Kyla to no end.

So, she and her foster sisters would have a lot to talk about. They needed to figure things out. What the future of the candy shop looked like, what the future of the house looked like. And what Frances's future looked like, as a widow with no biological family of her own. It was a tender subject.

Kyla felt her back stiffen as she gazed up at him. It was a small town, but this was really none of his business. She didn't care that he was the police chief, or that he had an obvious soft spot for Frances or that he looked good in that uniform. She wasn't going to chitchat like he was some kind of old friend, instead of the arrow in her heart that he absolutely was.

"I really should go," she said.

He nodded as she took another step back. His eyes said it all, even if he didn't utter the words. She wasn't going to be able to run away from him this time. After all, he worked right down the street.

"I'll be here if you need anything," he said. "And, Kyla…"

Reaching for the door, she turned.

He watched her, his shoulders hunched a little. His badge flashing in the sunlight that now bathed Main Street in its morning glow. "I'm sorry," he said. "About…all of it."

She paused for a second. Then retreated inside the sweet-smelling shop. *Me, too.*

"You take it plain, sweetie?" Frances called from the kitchen. "Or with sugar? I can't remember."

Kyla sat looking at the ocean from the cozy sunroom of the century-old three-story Victorian house that she'd called home since the sixth grade. The yard this time of year always reminded her of something out of a fairy tale—emerald-green grass, miniature roses, golden Scotch broom that grew in a wild, scattered way along the peeling picket fence. And the way the property ended in such unapologetic drama, hovering at the edge of a series of cliffs overlooking the blue-gray waters of the Pacific.

The fog and mist of the morning had given way to an early evening sunshine that warmed Kyla's face now. She leaned back in the old overstuffed chair that had always been her favorite reading spot as a kid, and smiled.

"Plain, Frances!" she called back. "Thanks."

It was good to be back. Like her sisters, she'd mostly stayed away, thinking she needed distance from her past. She thought if she had space, it would give her room to heal. But over the years, she'd begun to miss her foster mother terribly. Phone calls and short visits never filled the lonely crevices in her heart. So, in the end, making the choice to come home again hadn't been as complicated as she'd expected.

Now that she was here, though, she felt the significance all the way to her bones. *Home.* She was home. And what did that mean exactly? Something permanent? Or something that would end up slipping gently through her fingers like the sand on the beach?

Frances walked in carrying two glasses of iced tea with lemon wedges stuck in the rims.

"Here you go. Drink up, buttercup."

Her foster mother, wearing a Christmas Bay Middle School sweatshirt, since she was a proud Pirate booster, sat on the wicker chair across from Kyla, the sun making her bouffant blond hairdo glow platinum. She'd always been a beautiful woman, with smooth, luminous skin and big blue eyes, framed with thick lashes. Her eyes were what had drawn Kyla to her in the first place. What had made her trust again after not being able to trust very much at all.

They took her in now with their characteristic warmth. But there was a new sliver of vagueness in them that made Kyla's stomach knot. Frances was only sixty-two. Much too young to be losing her memory at such a fast pace. Her previous doctor had been leaning toward Alzheimer's, a devastating diagnosis, but Frances had stopped short of the tests that would confirm it. And then, had stopped going to the doctor altogether.

Ever since her husband had passed away, she'd had to make it on her own. She'd built Coastal Sweets into the successful business it was today, and had taken care of the lovely old house herself, which had been in her family for three generations.

In her own words, Frances did not have time for an Alzheimer's diagnosis. But of course, it wasn't that simple.

Kyla's heart swelled as she watched her take a sip of tea, and then set the glass down next to her cat, Jacques, who spent most weekdays at the candy shop curled up in a ridiculous pink bed beside the cash register. But he had today off, and was making the most of it by snoring away in a sunbeam.

Frances stroked his plump black-and-white belly, and he responded by stretching across the end table luxuriously, not bothering to open his eyes.

"So tell me again what happened with the chief?" Frances asked with a frown. "You said he caught a shoplifter?"

At the mention of Ben Martinez, Kyla's throat tightened. "Well, there was a shoplifter," she said. "But I haven't pressed charges. Not *yet*, anyway. I told him I'd think about it."

"Why?"

Kyla shrugged, taking a sip of her own tea. "You

know the type," she said, putting it down again. "Just looked a little lost and sad."

"I do know the type. But sometimes they need a wake-up call."

"That's true…"

Frances leaned back in the wicker chair, making it creak. "You know I'm a believer in tough love."

That *wasn't* quite true. Frances was a major softie deep down, but Kyla kept her mouth shut.

"Sometimes it's the very best thing," Frances continued. "But it's your call, honey. I worry about you in that shop all alone, though. Today it was only the tip jar, but what about tomorrow? I know when you were growing up here we never had to lock our doors, but things have changed. The town has changed. Things aren't nearly as safe as they used to be."

"I'm okay, Frances. Promise."

Frances touched the strand of freshwater pearls at her throat. A birthday present from Kyla during her first year of teaching. She'd wanted to get her something special, and they'd been in the window of their favorite boutique on the wharf.

"Even so," Frances said. "I'd feel better if I asked the chief to look in on you every now and then. Just in case."

"Ben?" She shook her head. "No way. I'll be fine. In fact, I'd rather take my chances with an armed robber."

"Honey…"

She shook her head again.

"Kyla Anne, look at me."

After a few seconds, Kyla did as she was told.

"When are you going to forgive that boy?" Frances asked quietly. "He was only doing what he thought was right. And he couldn't have known what would happen with your mom. He was just trying to protect you."

Kyla swallowed hard. In her heart, she knew that was true. But it still didn't change the fact that she'd never been allowed to go home again. That her mother had died alone. And Ben was the reason. Even if she wanted to, she didn't know *how* to forgive him.

"If it would make you feel better," she said, "you can ask him to come by. But I don't need—"

Frances held up a hand. "I know. You don't need his help."

"Well, I don't."

"Nobody says you do. Just do it for me?"

"You know I will."

"Oh, I know. I'm pretty good at getting what I want. How do you think I managed three teenage girls under one roof all those years?"

Kyla laughed.

Frances pointed a manicured finger at her, and took another sip of tea. Outside the open windows, there was the distant sound of waves lapping at the base of the cliffs. Gentle today, and not at all insistent like they'd be in the fall. The sun was at its most beautiful, slanting across the earth and hitting the water in thousands of golden sparkles that looked like sequins on a dress.

Leaning back, Kyla breathed in the salty air and listened to the gulls squabble in the yard. Maybe after dinner, they'd go for a walk on the beach. They hadn't gone hunting for agates since she'd been home.

Frances stroked Jacques again, and frowned. "What did you say happened with that shoplifter again? You didn't press charges?"

Kyla schooled her features, worried they'd betray the stab of pain in her heart. Instead, she reached for her foster mother's hand and smiled.

"No, Frances," she said. "I didn't."

Chapter Two

Ben sat at his desk, his head bent over the report. If Kyla decided to give Hunter a break, it'd probably be one of the first the kid ever got. He'd had a hard road. Which by all accounts, led right back to his dad.

Gabe Mohatt's rap sheet was a mile long. Domestics, mostly. But there were some assaults in there, too. Some thefts, a disturbing the peace and one urinating in a public place. *Father of the Year.* Ben couldn't help feeling for his son, who despite everything, seemed genuinely sorry for his attempted theft at the candy shop the other day.

Sighing, he leaned back and closed the file. When Frances had called asking him to look in on Kyla, he'd told her he was happy to. It was a small town, and he'd do the same for anyone else. But the truth was, it had taken nearly all his willpower not to head over to the shop first thing that morning. And that had less to do with the fact that he thought she needed looking in on, and more to do with his need to see her again. To see how she was (*Liar. You want to see if she still hates you*) after everything that had happened.

And this had him unsettled.

"Daddy, can we go visit Jacques now?"

Ben glanced up at his daughter, who looked so small and out of place in the cool blues and grays of the police department that he had to smile. She was wearing her favorite unicorn T-shirt, which twinkled under the fluorescent lighting. Tabitha, her babysitter, had an appointment this morning, so she'd come in to work with him for a while. Which was fine. Gracie was used to it—she'd spent a good part of her babyhood in an ExerSaucer in the corner of his office.

Ben was a single dad, but he was also the chief, which meant he got to make up some of the rules as he went along. He wasn't going to lie; that part was nice. Under his leadership, the department had turned into a family friendly workplace, with lots of flexibility for parents. There was even a playroom in the back where kids could be for short periods of time, if needed. He liked to think he would've done that for his officers anyway, but the truth was, raising his daughter on his own had given him a unique perspective. And a much bigger understanding than he might've had otherwise.

He rubbed the stubble on his chin. He'd skipped shaving this morning in lieu of making pancakes in the shape of cat heads. Gracie's favorite. He'd promised, and she never let him worm his way out of a promise, even if it meant spending the day looking like he'd just rolled out of bed.

"I don't know if he's there today, honey," he said. "Frances has been keeping him home more since it's busier in the shop now. She doesn't want him getting out like he did last summer."

Gracie brushed her dark bangs out of her eyes. They were still a little crooked. Ben had trimmed them himself, a huge mistake that Isabel had ribbed him about for days. But Gracie didn't seem to care. She had a one-track mind. *Cat.*

"He just wanted to explore," she said matter-of-factly. "And he needed the exercise, anyways. He's a chunk."

She sounded exactly like Frances when she said this. Jacques was, indeed, a chunk.

He smiled. "Yes, but he still can't go outside. No matter how bored he gets, or how much cardio he needs."

"What's cardio?"

"It's when you move really fast and your heart beats fast, too."

"Like when you go to the gym and get all sweaty?"

"Just like that."

"Why would you want your heart to beat fast?"

"It makes it stronger. And the stronger it is, the better off you are."

She nodded, seeming to contemplate this. "If you do a lot of cardio, does that mean your heart won't get broken so easy?"

He pushed away from his desk and stood. It was Saturday, so he was the only one on duty until this afternoon. Which was a good thing, because Gracie could talk a person's ear off. This morning, her usual chatter wasn't keeping anyone from their work but him.

"It doesn't really work that way, sweetie," he said. "But I wish it did."

"Because Aunt Isabel said her heart is broken for Frances."

The radio on his duty belt crackled as the dispatcher responded to a deputy in the next town over. Frowning, he turned it down. "Why's that?"

"She said she's all alone. But I told her she has Jacques."

"She absolutely does," Ben said, reaching for her hand. It was soft and warm. A little sticky. He wondered how long exactly, that a little girl would want to hold her dad's hand. He hoped it would be a long time.

They headed toward the department's glass front doors, and the bright summer morning outside. "She has Jacques," he continued, "and she has us, too. And now she has a nice lady who came back to help her with the candy shop. She used to live with Frances when she was little. You'll get to meet her when we say hi to Jacques."

Gracie grinned. Gap-toothed and cute as hell. But of course, he was biased.

"What's her name?"

He pushed the door open, making sure it was locked behind them. There was an official sign in the window for the tourists, but locals knew to call Dispatch if the doors were locked. The department was just too small to justify a receptionist on the weekends.

"Her name is Kyla," he said. "And I used to know her when I was a kid. So did Aunt Isabel."

"Why did she move away?"

Ben squeezed her hand, thinking carefully before he answered. Gracie was at the age where everything you said to her, or in *front* of her, got right back to whoever you were talking about in record time. He'd learned this the hard way.

"You know how Jacques got out last summer?" he said.

She nodded, skipping next to him.

"I think it might've been like that for Kyla, too. I think Christmas Bay might've been a little too small for her, and she needed to explore."

"And she needed some cardio?"

"Not exactly."

"Look!" Gracie pointed to the Coastal Sweets sign hanging over the sidewalk in the distance. "The doors are closed! I bet that means Jacques is there today, Daddy. I bet that means they're closed so he won't get out."

Ben felt his heartbeat pick up inside his chest, feeling as though he'd done some cardio himself. Still having a hard time with the fact that Kyla Beckett, very grown, and now very beautiful, was back in town. And not only that, she clearly hated him and the horse he rode in on, too.

Ben was a realist. He was also a cop, who was used to making decisions that people didn't like. But when he'd told his high school counselor that Kyla wasn't being looked after by her mother, he'd only been a kid. Seventeen years old, too young to grasp the full ramifications of his actions. He'd gone to his parents first, but they had been hesitant to get involved in her situation at home, and it was only later that he understood they must have known very well what might happen to their daughter's friend. Whereas Ben hadn't realized how that day would change Kyla's life moving forward. He'd only acted on instinct, on the spur of the moment. He'd just wanted to make sure she was safe. That she was okay.

And now, all these years later, he found himself wanting to explain this to her. Whether she was open to hearing it or not.

Gracie pulled her hand out of his, and ran up ahead, her hair shining in the sun. He wanted to tell her to slow down, to be careful, or she might fall. Gracie was only five years younger than Kyla had been when she'd been taken away from her mom. Ben's chest tightened at the thought. What would've happened if he hadn't said anything that day? Could he have lived with himself? He didn't think so. He remembered her worn-out clothes. How on sleepovers with Isabel, she'd eaten like she was ravenous, and then asked to take the leftovers home. He remembered her skinned knees—raw and bruised. As though nobody had been there to tell her to slow down. Nobody had picked her up when she'd fallen.

And all of a sudden, he knew he'd do it all over again.

Kyla straightened the lid on the black licorice bin, the tangy smell filling her senses and bringing her right back to her childhood. She used to hate black licorice. Now she loved it. Apparently, it was an acquired taste.

She looked around the shop, which sparkled from the scrubbing she'd just given it. She'd mopped the old hardwood floors until they shone. She'd cleaned all the windows (she had no idea how many little fingerprints could accumulate on a window until she'd come to work in a candy shop). And she'd wiped down all the bins, which came in a close second to the windows in the fingerprint department.

Glancing over at Jacques, who was busy giving himself a bath in his princess bed, she smiled. "Ready for the day, Beau?"

He blinked at her through yellow eyes, not looking particularly ready for anything. Unless it was a nap.

The front door opened with a tinkle of the bell above it, and she turned to greet her first customer of the morning.

A little girl bounded inside. Beautiful, with big brown eyes, and a T-shirt with rainbow sequins all over it. Her bangs were jagged, with one side drooping lower than the other, and Kyla smiled down at her, assuming she'd probably tried giving herself a haircut.

"Well, hi there," she said.

"Hi!" The little girl beamed up at Kyla, her tongue clearly visible between a gap in her front teeth.

"Are you here all by yourself?"

"Nope. My dad is coming, but he's kind of slow. Because he's old."

"Ahh."

She bounced on her purple sneakers a few times, then turned her attention to Jacques, who had the good manners to stop licking his rear end.

"Aww, hi there, little fella," the girl cooed. "Are you all cozy in your bed?"

With a hoarse purr, the cat began making biscuits like he was behind on an order. He was in his element.

Kyla smiled and leaned against the counter. "Do you know Jacques?"

"I sure do. He's my favorite kitty in the whole world. Aren't you, buddy?"

Jacques gazed at her as if this was a foregone conclusion.

"Well," Kyla said, "he definitely likes you. I don't
think I've ever heard him purr that loud. He sounds
like a motorboat, doesn't he?"

The little girl giggled, and scratched under his
chin. He closed his eyes and stretched his neck out
in feline ecstasy. Definitely in his wheelhouse.

The door opened behind them with another tinkle
of the bell, and Kyla turned expecting to see an older
gentleman who belonged to this sweetheart. Maybe
even a grandpa-type, who had a hard time keeping
up with his child that he'd had later on in life.

She smiled wide. And then felt it wilt on her lips.
The man walking through the door was most certainly not a grandpa-type. And looked more than
capable of keeping up with anyone or anything in
that uniform.

Ben...

He put his hands in his pockets and let his smoky
gaze settle on her. Looking completely unaffected
by the sudden vibes she knew she was putting out.

So, this little girl was his. Of course she was. Now,
it was totally obvious—the dark hair and eyes, the
fact that she seemed at home in the candy shop, and
with Jacques in particular. Kyla remembered Frances
saying he had a daughter, that he stopped by a lot for
gummy worms, her favorite. *Great.* Now she had to
be civil. At least in front of his adorable offspring.

She knew Frances was fretting about her being

alone in the shop, but couldn't she have had someone else check in on her? Like a community service officer or something? Someone who drove a golf cart and gave out tickets for double-parking?

Kyla raised her chin. The truth was, she'd agree to just about anything to put Frances's mind at ease, but she was just fine running the shop on her own. She didn't need Ben Martinez's help with anything. He looked so…*smug* standing there with that scruff on his jaw. With that warmth in his eyes that was making her stomach dip, despite her willing it not to. He looked like he could scoop her up in his arms and carry her off somewhere, like some damsel in distress.

And, yeah. Okay. Maybe she'd been in love with those kinds of books as a preteen, and maybe she'd fantasized about Ben more than she'd care to admit. But that was before. Before she'd grown. Before she'd changed.

"Good morning," she said evenly, aware that his daughter was watching her now. And watching her dad, too. With interest.

"Good morning."

"I was just talking to your daughter. Who's delightful, by the way."

He reached down and put a hand on his little girl's head. "Thank you. She got away from me down the sidewalk, and then I ran into a guy from the fire department." He smiled. "Small town. Gotta talk."

Kyla looked down at his hand. *No ring.* Maybe he

was married and just didn't wear one. Or maybe he was single. A thought that shouldn't have mattered to her in the least, but it wiggled its way into her subconscious anyway. He had his daughter with him at work. Where was her mother? And all of a sudden, Kyla's throat squeezed. She understood what it was like being little and not having your mom around.

Reaching into a nearby jar, she grabbed a Tootsie Pop.

"Want one?" she asked, offering it to the little girl. "From Jacques. He's the candy shop mascot. Has to keep his customers happy."

"What do you say, Gracie?" Ben said.

"Thank you!"

"I should've introduced you two earlier," he said. "Honey, this is Kyla."

The sound of her name coming from that wide, expressive mouth gave her butterflies. She remembered the way he used to say it when she was a kid, part of why she'd had that massive crush on him. He'd always sounded so capable. Whatever Isabel's big brother said, went.

He'd obviously carried that presence with him into adulthood, and the career he'd chosen for himself. She didn't know much about him now, but she did know he was probably a very good police officer. That part was clear.

She bent down so she was eye to eye with his daughter. Gracie. Such a pretty name.

"I'm pleased to meet you," she said.

Gracie offered a dainty hand. "I'm very pleased to meet you, too," she said primly. Like maybe she'd watched one too many princess movies.

Kyla straightened again, letting her gaze fall to Ben's badge. Remembering that he might've come in to get Gracie some gummy worms, but he was also here in an official capacity, too. And as a favor to Frances.

She cleared her throat. "I know Frances asked you to come by," she said. "But you don't have to worry. I'm doing great."

"That's good to know. But that's not the only reason I'm here. I was also going to ask if you'd made up your mind about those charges yet."

"Oh. Well, I don't think I'm going to press any. Not this time, anyway."

"You're sure about that?"

She frowned. "I thought I was…"

"I get it. He's just a kid. But he also has a history of shoplifting and petty theft in the area. You should probably keep an eye on that tip jar. Just in case."

She let that settle. He was right. She needed to be prepared for anything. Especially for pressing charges if there was ever another run-in with Hunter Mohatt. Sad eyes, or no.

So, she guessed she was going to listen to Christmas Bay's chief of police. The one with the rugged scruff and the cute daughter, and the hand without the wedding ring. And she guessed she was going to let him help her. At least a little. But that didn't mean she'd forgive him, or even like him again. It just meant that she was a grown-up now, and so was he, and they'd be working right down the street from each other, and this was what grown-ups did.

Gracie bounced on her toes, looking like she was ready to get this show on the road. "Daddy," she said. "Gummy worms?"

"Sure. Just a small bag, okay?"

She turned to Kyla with a sudden sparkle in her eyes. "You should come down to the police department and see my daddy's office. I can show you all around, and I can share my worms with you."

Kyla grinned. It was impossible not to. "Well, that sounds super nice, but I have to be here to run the shop. Jacques can't work the cash register." She wiggled her fingers. "No thumbs."

Gracie laughed. "No thumbs!"

Jacques stretched from his bed on the countertop, as if caring that he heard his name.

"We should get out of your hair," Ben said, digging a few dollars from his pocket. Taut muscles slid underneath the tanned skin of his forearms. "And I need to go let Hunter know he's off the hook. After I make him listen to my speech on good behavior, of course."

He winked at her, which did funny things to her resolve. *Nope.* She was not going to get sucked into that old charm. No matter how much her body was fighting her on it. No matter how much her heart remembered him.

Ben Martinez was trouble. And she and trouble had parted ways a long time ago.

The road out to Hunter's house was full of potholes, and Ben had to keep slowing his cruiser down in order to avoid the worst of them. He rocked over one now, silently cursing the evening fog. This wasn't doing his suspension any good.

He was supposed to have been off a few hours ago, but he'd had to wait for Tabitha to pick Gracie up in order to finish this business with Hunter. He could've done it tomorrow, but he knew that if he had any hopes of making an impact on this kid, their talk needed to happen sooner rather than later. Hunter was only fifteen, but he was clearly on the precipice of a very hard life if he didn't start making better choices soon. And all of a sudden, Ben thought of Kyla—growing up in a neighborhood not unlike this one, with the dilapidated houses and the road out front that seemed to lead nowhere.

Frowning, he craned his neck and looked out the window, trying to read the addresses as he passed. And then, in a driveway up ahead, he recognized Gabe Mohatt's truck—a lifted black Ford that he'd pulled over more than once.

Ben eased up to the curb, put the cruiser into Park and cued his mic.

"Forty-seven twenty-one."

"Forty-seven twenty-one," the dispatcher replied through the static. "Go ahead."

"I'll be out at two zero eight Ocean Vista Drive on a follow-up."

"Copy that."

Ben cut the engine and got out of the car, struck by how quiet it was. No dogs barking or running around loose. No kids playing before dark. He glanced up at the living room window, where someone was peering through the slats in the blinds. When they saw him, the blinds snapped shut again.

Uneasy, he looked around. This was only supposed to be a follow-up to a shoplifting case, but he'd been doing this too long to ignore the hairs prickling on the back of his neck.

He made his way to the front door, where he knocked, then waited. After a few seconds, a weary-looking woman opened it, and he could immediately smell some kind of meat cooking from the kitchen.

"Ma'am," he said. "I'm Chief Martinez with Christmas Bay PD. I hope I'm not interrupting your dinner, but I'm here to talk to Hunter. Are you his mother?"

She sighed. "Yes, I'm Stacey. What's he done now?"

Normally, he'd just come right out with it. But something about the look on her face, about the feeling of the house in general, made him choose his words carefully.

"I tried getting in touch with you yesterday," he said. "There was an incident in town—" Her mouth dropped, and he held up a hand. "Nothing huge. But

I do need to talk to him if he's here. And you, if it's a good time. Otherwise, I'll need you to bring him down to the station."

He added that last part for effect. In case she decided she didn't want to deal with her son's issues right then. Or at all, for that matter.

She looked at him, and he smiled back, wanting to put her at ease. But more than that, wanting her on his side, so he had a better chance of helping her kid.

"Hunter," she called. "Come in here, please."

After a minute, he appeared, wearing a rumpled T-shirt and ripped jeans. When he saw Ben, his expression fell. He looked even younger than he had yesterday.

"This is Chief Martinez," his mom said. "But it sounds like you two already know each other?"

"Oh. Hi."

Obviously, he hadn't mentioned stealing the tip jar to his mother. He kept glancing nervously toward the living room, like he was expecting someone to appear any minute.

"Hunter went into Coastal Sweets yesterday morning," Ben said evenly, "and took the tip jar from the counter."

Stacey rubbed her temple.

"He got lucky. They aren't going to press charges, so I'm just here to give him a warning."

Hunter was now staring up at him with surprisingly wide eyes. This kid may have been around the block a few times, but the effect of having a uniformed police officer at his front door wasn't lost on him, either. That was a good thing. And exactly what Ben had been hoping for. Right now, tip money and candy bars weren't going to land him in jail. But in a few years he might graduate to something that might.

"I know this kind of thing seems small to you right now, Hunter," he said. "But there are implications. Ripple effects that go farther than you think. You're a smart kid—I can tell. You've got a lot of potential. You don't want people thinking you're trouble every time they see you coming."

Hunter looked down and worried the hem of his T-shirt between his fingers. His mop of blond hair hung in his eyes and it was impossible to tell what he was thinking right then. But Ben had a pretty good idea.

"I can see that you're sorry," he said, his voice low. "So why did you do it?"

The answer was important. It was an opportunity for Hunter to own this. To face it, even if it was only for a minute or two.

The boy shrugged, his shoulders angular and sharp underneath his T-shirt. "It's better than being ignored, I guess."

Ben felt his heart beat heavily inside his chest. *And there it is...*

Before he could reply, Gabe Mohatt walked in behind Hunter. He narrowed his pale blue eyes at his wife, as if she'd been keeping something from him. Then shifted his gaze to Ben, where it settled with obvious hostility.

"What's going on here?" he snapped.

Ben cleared his throat, not liking his tone. Actually, not liking anything about him. And knowing that if he left him in a foul mood, his family would probably pay the price.

"Hunter took something the other day," Ben said, "and I just came by to give him a warning. We had a talk, and I think that's all I need from you folks tonight."

"Took something? You mean stole."

Hunter stared at the floor. All the color had drained from his face, leaving the scattered pimples on his cheeks red as cherries.

"Nobody's pressing charges," Ben said. "This is just a warning."

Gabe flicked Hunter in the back of the head. "Lucky for you."

"Hey," Ben said. "Everything's fine. He's not going to do it again, are you?"

"You can leave now, Martinez." Gabe said. "He's *my* boy—I'll handle it."

The insinuation was clear. He was the parent, and there was only so much Ben could do here, police chief or no. And honestly, the longer he stayed, the more agitated Gabe would get.

Forcing a calmness into his expression that he definitely didn't feel, Ben looked down at Hunter. "If you have any questions, give me a call, okay?"

And then he walked out the door. Hoping the kid would keep his act clean from here on out. But knowing the odds of that weren't exactly great.

Chapter Three

Kyla stepped onto the treadmill and looked around the small gym. So far, she was the only one here, which suited her just fine. It had been roughly a decade since she'd been on one of these things, and quite frankly, she was worried it was going to catapult her off, and right into the wall behind her.

Reaching up, she pulled her Mariners cap low over her eyes, while a light rain pattered against the windows outside. Walking on the beach before work would always be her favorite way to get her steps in, but she'd never been much of a trouper in the rain. Plus, the zipper was broken on her raincoat, so the treadmill it was. Frances was excited about the family membership she'd just bought, just in case any of "her girls" wanted to use it when they came to visit. Which was so sweet. And so Frances.

Kyla let her gaze fall to the dozen or so red-and-green lights that were flashing at her, as if losing their patience. Frowning, she started punching buttons trying to find the brisk walk setting. She'd save the level ten, vertical, mountaineer badass setting for another day.

The door across the gym opened with a soft swoosh, but she didn't look up. She was too busy trying to program her weight in. And then trying to bypass the weight setting altogether.

Someone put their bag down next to the free weights, and she caught the faintest scent of aftershave. Or maybe it was men's deodorant. Whatever it was, it smelled good. It reminded her of high school, and passing the boys in the hallway, all freshly showered from their morning wrestling practice. Of course, none of those boys had ever known she existed. Not that she cared. Her heart had already been taken, and then crushed, by the time she'd walked through the doors as a gangly freshman at Christmas Bay High School.

Frustrated with all the buttons, and at the treadmill's complete lack of sympathy for her, she sighed.

"Right?" said a male voice behind her. "I miss the old ones where you just had to push Start."

She looked into the mirror, ready to smile at the stranger behind her. Ready to commiserate over all things treadmill. Only, after a second, she realized this wasn't any stranger.

Ben Martinez leaned against a stair-stepper, looking completely at ease in the gym environment. Mostly because of his body, and how many muscles bulged underneath his plain white T-shirt. Which, by the way, looked amazing on him.

She let out an even breath. He had a way of doing this to her. Showing up out of nowhere, and reminding her of things she'd rather not be reminded of. Like how it felt to be in his presence. Safe, cared for. Watched over.

"I thought that was you when I walked in," he said. "But you were concentrating so hard, I didn't want to bother you."

She adjusted her hat that didn't really need adjusting. Just so she had something to do with her hands. "I think this thing might be smarter than I am."

He grinned. "Never."

"I don't know. I'm still standing here, not moving."

"Want me to take a look?"

Did she? Not really. At that moment, having him any closer than he already was seemed like a fairly bad idea. He smelled good. Looked even better. And there was no denying that she now had butterflies. *Perfect.*

But right then, she couldn't think of any plausible reason she could decline his offer. Especially since it didn't seem like she was going to figure it out on her own. At least not before Thanksgiving, and she really didn't want to be stuck in the gym that long.

She shrugged, trying to appear nonchalant. *Sure! Take a look. Take three looks, doesn't matter to me!*

Only, it did, and she took a small step back as he stepped forward. And then leaned over her to reach the offending buttons.

"Here's your problem," he said. "You have to hit menu first, and then the back arrow to get to the settings."

She only heard part of that. Something about the menu button. She'd let her gaze settle on the back of his neck, where his dark hair was cut neatly, but not too short. It curled inward toward his ears—just enough for her to imagine how it'd look in a few weeks if he let it grow. Black and shiny and incredibly sexy.

"Is that what you want to do?" he asked, looking at her over his shoulder.

"Do I...what?"

His mouth tilted slightly. Teasingly. It was possible he knew exactly what she'd been thinking right then. He seemed pretty intuitive, and she was rotten at hiding her feelings. Always had been.

"Do you want to skip the workout settings?"

She nodded.

He pushed a few more buttons, and the lights stopped blinking. The treadmill went blessedly dark, looking for the most part like it wouldn't try anything hinky. Like launch her into the stratosphere.

He leaned back again, and it was almost like his warmth went with him. She could feel it moving away, and something deep inside her, something instinctive, wanted to reach out and pull it back.

"If I eat any more of Gracie's gummy worms," he said, "I'll have to come down here more often."

She felt herself relax at the mention of his daughter and her gummy worms. They were a much safer thought than Ben and his body heat.

"How's she doing?" she asked. "She'll have to come in to see Jacques again. He loves the attention."

"She's okay. The summers can be long for her with me working all the time, and her mother not—" He stopped short, and the muscles in his jaw bunched.

Kyla waited. She'd wondered about Gracie's mom. Wondered if she was in the picture or not. If Ben was single, maybe it was because he had to be, and not because he wanted to be.

Rubbing his chin, he looked away for a minute. This close, she could see that his lashes were impossibly long for a man. He was like that. Impossible in nearly every way.

"Well, it's just hard for her," he finished, his voice low.

"I get it. You don't have to explain."

Maybe there was insinuation in her voice that she hadn't intended, but he looked down at her right then. She looked back, and his eyes seemed to pin her in place. She reached for the handrail on the treadmill, suddenly a little dizzy. The truth was, she understood exactly what it felt like to be without a mother. And if Gracie was experiencing even a little of that unique kind of pain, Kyla was very sorry for her.

But she hadn't intended to let Ben see into her so easily.

"I know you do," Ben finally said. "I know it was hard for you, too."

She licked her lips, not knowing exactly what to say to that. In all her daydreams about Ben since junior high, she'd always imagined confronting him. Demanding to know why he couldn't have just left her with her mother? Even though she was grown now, that anger was still there. The confusion and hurt. She'd never found a way to move past it. To move past *him*.

Today, she didn't trust herself with asking him anything. She was too moved by his presence, to drawn to him physically, to be able to untangle any of this in her mind and heart. It was just going to have to wait for another day. Or maybe forever.

He seemed to sense her withdrawing into herself, into the memories, and he walked back over to the weights. Probably wanting to give her space. Not wanting to push, which she had to give him credit for.

"I went to see Hunter Mohatt, by the way," he said. "To let him know you weren't pressing charges, and to give him an official warning."

He bent down to grab a towel from his duffel bag. His legs were muscular and smooth underneath his athletic shorts, and she imagined what the rest of his body looked like before she could help it.

She cleared her throat. She'd almost forgotten about Hunter this morning, and was glad he'd mentioned it.

"What did he say?" she asked.

"He seemed sorry enough. I like him, even though he really hasn't given me any reason to yet."

"I know what you mean. I got that from him, too. He reminds me of me at that age."

"You were never a hoodlum," he said.

"No, but I had my own things going on. Well… you know."

It was the elephant in the room. It was also the first time she'd ever admitted to Ben that there'd been anything wrong at home. She'd basically spent her entire childhood defending her mother, shielding her from everyone else's judgment. Even if that judgment had been more than warranted. And when he'd asked her back then if everything was okay, she'd lied and said it was. Even now, it was hard to get anything else past her lips.

Kyla turned away then and punched the Start button on the treadmill. But not before she snuck a look at Ben in the mirror behind her. He was watching her with an unreadable expression on his face. Her belly tightened, and she had to force herself to look away. In those eyes, she could see the boy he'd been. The boy who'd done his best to protect her. But that protection had come at a terrible price.

After a minute, he lay down on the weight bench, and positioned himself underneath the bar. "He doesn't have a good home life," he said, picking it up and resting it across his chest. "His dad is pretty rough. I just hope some of what I said got through, or I can see him ending up the same way."

Kyla pushed the Arrow Up button to increase the speed on the treadmill. Then planted her hands on the rails and began walking in earnest. Once upon a time, Frances had been worried she would end up just like her mother. And she wasn't the only one. Teachers, counselors, friends—even Stella and Marley had been concerned for her. Just like she understood what it felt like to be a kid like Gracie who was without one of her parents, she understood what it was like to be a kid like Hunter, who was linked by DNA to trouble and doubt. It wasn't easy.

Pulling her baseball cap farther over her eyes, she resisted the urge to look over at Ben again, instead, watching the rain trickle down the windows.

"Coming!" Ben called toward the front door. Then tripped over Gracie's favorite stuffed animal that she'd left in the hallway. He'd almost broken his neck on Henry the Hippo more than once. He swore under his breath.

"Daddy, where are you going?" Gracie croaked from her bedroom.

"I told Aunt Isabel about your tummy, so she stopped by on her way home to take a look at you. No big deal." He added that last part to ease his daughter's anxiety. She was scared to death of needles, and knew very well that her aunt wielded them at work. She had a healthy skepticism whenever Isabel just wanted to "take a look." Even though Gracie had never gotten a shot anywhere other than at her own pediatrician's office.

Ben unlocked the dead bolt and yanked the door open.

Isabel stood on his stoop, covering her head with a magazine as the rain dripped on her shoulders. Her brown eyes were teasing. As a mother, she was pretty much unflappable. Ben was anything but. He was a worrier, and this entertained Isabel to no end.

"You look a little frazzled, big brother," she said, stepping past him into the foyer. "Take a breath."

"I have," he said. "I am. But I googled it, and it really does sound like appendicitis this time. Those can pop."

She smiled patiently. "You're right, they can. But she's not in enough pain for that. If it *was* her appendix, which I doubt it is, it wouldn't be about to burst."

Ben helped her out of her coat and shook it, before hanging it by the door. Her shoulder-length black hair was damp at the ends, her pink blouse looking cheerful and bright in the dim light of the ranch house. He'd just picked Gracie up from Tabitha's, and he'd barely turned on any lights when the stomach pains had started. He'd been kneeling by her canopy bed ever since.

"Ben, I love you dearly," Isabel said, "but you've got to relax. Every stomachache does not an appendectomy make."

"Ahh. You're a poet and didn't know it."

She laughed.

He had to admit, he'd cried wolf a few times. Once on Halloween when Gracie had eaten half a bag of Twix when he hadn't been looking, and once in the spring when she'd caught a tummy bug that was going around.

"In my defense," he said, "I don't think Sam ever called the doctor enough."

Isabel's shoulders stiffened. "Sam didn't do a lot of things enough. Like sticking around for her husband and child."

"Wow. You don't pull any punches, do you?"

"For her? Why should I?"

"Remind me not to get on your bad side."

"Never."

"Even when I beg for house calls?"

"These aren't house calls," Isabel said. "They're just…visits."

Ben smiled. "Right."

"Where is she?"

"In her bed. Looking pretty miserable at the moment."

Ben followed his sister down the hall and into Gracie's room.

"What's going on, munchkin?" Isabel asked, bending down to feel Gracie's forehead for a temperature.

Gracie scooted up, perkier than when Ben had left her a minute ago.

"I think it was just a gas bubble," she announced matter-of-factly.

"Oh?"

"Frances gets them, too."

"She does?"

"Yeah. When she eats something that doesn't agree with her."

"Did you eat something that didn't agree with you?"

"No. Just a hot dog at Tabitha's house."

"Oh."

"And some cookies after."

"Okay…" Isabel said.

"And the rest of my worms from the other day."

"When did you have those?" Ben asked, incredulous.

"In the car."

Isabel glanced at him over her shoulder.

"It was a long day," he said. "I was preoccupied." He didn't mention what he was preoccupied with, and that was the memory of Kyla at the gym that morning. In sweats and a T-shirt. Nothing jaw-droppingly scandalous or fashionable, maybe, but he'd still had a hard time taking his eyes off her.

Isabel looked back at Gracie and smoothed her bangs away from her forehead. "I think our mystery is solved. But I'd go easy on any snacks tonight, okay?"

Gracie nodded, then turned to Ben. "Sorry, Daddy."

"It's okay, honey. I'm just glad you're feeling better."

"Me, too. Gas bubbles are the pits."

Another Frances favorite. Gracie was full of them.

Ben dug his phone out from his uniform shirt pocket and handed it to her. "Here. You can play *Animal Crossing* for a few minutes while I visit with Aunt Isabel, okay?"

Her face lit up. He tried his best to limit her screen time, so playing on his phone was still a treat. He wondered how long he'd be able to keep it that way. Most of the kids in her class already had their own iPhones, or iPads or both.

Isabel leaned down to kiss her niece on the cheek, and was rewarded with a squeeze around the neck. When Gracie was settled in with her game, they headed into the kitchen where Ben turned on the coffeepot.

"Just a quick cup," he said. "I know you've got to get home, but we should catch up a little. I haven't seen you for days."

His sister pulled out a stool at the island and wiggled up. She was so petite that her feet didn't touch the floor. Ben used to tease her about it, but got tired of being punched in the gut, so he'd learned to keep his mouth shut.

"Coffee sounds great," she said. "It's so wet out there. I've been cold all day."

"It's supposed to rain until Wednesday." He took off his duty belt, and put it in a locking cabinet next to the stove. Then pulled out a stool next to Isabel. "I don't mind it, though. I like the rain."

"I know. Remember making those disgusting mud pies when we were kids? I'm surprised we didn't all end up with pneumonia."

He smiled. "Poor Mom."

"But we had it good, though. The best childhood, right?"

The coffee began to percolate, the comforting scent filling Ben's senses. And something about the rain coming down, the talk of their childhood, brought the memories back until they were thick as beach grass in front of his eyes. The Martinez kids had it good, no doubt. They'd been loved by their parents; they'd never known what it was like to go to bed hungry, or want for anything, ever.

He rested his elbows on the counter. Then steepled his fingers like he was getting ready to interrogate someone. Habit. "Kyla Beckett is back in town," he said quietly.

Isabel looked over at him, her eyes wide. "To stay?"

"She got here a few weeks ago to help Frances at Coastal Sweets. I think she's planning on being here for the summer."

"You've seen her, then?"

Her tone was unmistakable. Even though Isabel hadn't seen Kyla in years, she still cared about her. They'd been inseparable as girls, only really growing apart when Kyla had been taken from her mother's home. Isabel had known Kyla had been angry and hurt, and had followed their parents' advice to give her time and space. The months had grown into years, and now here they were.

"She had a shoplifter the other day, and Frances asked me to look in on her."

Isabel swiveled on her stool to face him. "Well? What did she say? How is she? How does she look?"

He held up a hand. "Whoa, whoa. I only talked to her for a few minutes."

"Jeez, Ben. You're terrible at this."

"At nosing into people's lives?"

"This is Kyla we're talking about here."

"Yes, but it's been a while, Isabel. Almost twenty damn years. She's an adult now. Plus, she hates me."

"She can't hate you."

"Trust me. She does."

Isabel frowned. "Well, she just doesn't know you. As an adult, anyway."

"She knows enough."

"You were only a kid. You did the right thing. She was being neglected."

"You know that, and I know that, but I'm not sure she's come to terms with it yet. If how she looks at me is any indication. And really, she has every right to feel the way she does. The whole thing was a mess."

Isabel sat up straight, a determined look settling over her face. "I'm going to go see her."

"I thought you might."

"I'll cook for her. Her favorite things."

"They were her favorites when she was *ten*."

Isabel ignored that. "Comfort food," she said. I'll make it just like Mom did. A welcome back to Christmas Bay, we still love you, you can't stay mad forever…kind of thing."

Ben wished he could argue with this, but honestly, Kyla would probably be happy to see Isabel again. Everyone loved his sister. It was impossible not to.

Isabel gazed up at him then, her eyebrows scrunched together. "Well, how does she look? You can at least tell me that part. She was always so tiny, Kyla. Remember how tiny she was? So thin. And those glasses…"

He felt his neck heat. All of a sudden, he felt the need to loosen his collar. "No glasses."

"And?"

"And…and what?"

"Ben. This isn't that hard." Isabel looked annoyed. Then, slowly, she smiled. "Oh. I get it."

He didn't say anything. Just got off the stool to grab a couple of mugs from the cupboard, making sure to keep his back turned.

"She must be pretty," Isabel said behind him. "You're so easy to read. Honestly."

"And you're a pain in my ass."

"So, she's pretty. Is she single?"

"How would I know?" he said, pouring coffee into one mug, and then the other. The steam curled into the air as the rain outside pattered against the kitchen window.

"You could always ask."

He turned around and gave her a look. "I told you. She hates me."

Isabel waved him away. "Tiny detail."

"Listen," Ben said, sitting back down beside her. "I know nothing about this woman except for how she was as a kid. She's probably only going to be here for the summer, and she's got her hands full with Frances and the shop."

"And she's pretty." Isabel wrapped her hands around the mug and took a sip of coffee. "Just saying."

Ben took a sip too, burning his tongue. "Shit," he muttered.

"Just admit that it might be time to jump back into dating. You've been divorced for two years."

"And when, exactly, would I have time for a new relationship? Besides, Sam ruined me."

"Oh, don't be so dramatic."

"You were the one who was just reminding me how awful she was."

"She was awful," Isabel said. "She was a lousy wife and mother. Obviously. But that doesn't mean *all* women are lousy."

Ben took another sip of his coffee and pondered that. No, that was true. And not all relationships would end up leaving a trail of scorched earth in their wake, either. But the reality was, Gracie had been so traumatized by her mother leaving, that he didn't think he could trust anyone with her heart again.

As for his heart? It was going to take a lot more

than looks to be able to open it after the way his marriage had ended. Speaking of scorched earth.

Isabel put her coffee down and touched his shoulder. "Hey."

He looked over.

"I'm sorry," she said. "I don't mean to bring up bad memories—you know that. I just want you to be happy. You deserve some happiness. Gracie does, too. You've got so much to offer someone, Ben."

"That's me—the bachelor of Christmas Bay," he said, his lips tilting. "With a six-year-old daughter, and a buttload of trust issues."

"You're so cynical."

"Only being honest."

"And I'm just saying, Kyla could use a friend here. Or two. I'm not going to matchmake—I promise. I'll just bring her a peace offering, and if that paves the way for some friendly, neighborhood chats with our amazing police chief, well then…"

There was no use arguing. When Isabel made up her mind, it usually took an act of God to change it. And even then it could be a struggle.

"Listen," she said, looking at her watch, "it's bath time, and if I know Jason, he's probably letting the boys fill water balloons up in the tub. I'd better run."

Ben stood up and pulled his little sister into a hug. "Thanks for coming. I promise it'll be appendicitis next time. For real."

Isabel laughed. "I hope not! But it might be time for a gummy worm intervention."

"Easier said than done."

She tapped his badge. "You're the boss. Just stick to you guns."

"Whatever you say."

"See? That wasn't so hard. It's about time you started listening to me."

"Don't get used to it."

She stood on her tiptoes and kissed him on the cheek. "I'll call you in a few days. Give the munchkin a squeeze for me."

Ben helped with her coat, then stood in the doorway and watched her run to her car in the rain. When she was buckled up, she started the engine and waved, pulling away with the headlights cutting into the gray of the evening.

Slowly, he closed the door, and then stood there with his hands in his pockets. He gritted his teeth, feeling the muscles in his jaw bunch almost painfully. That's what he got for thinking about Sam, for letting her back in again.

Since she'd left, he'd kept his head down. He'd gone to work, tried to make his job count, tried to be the best dad he could be to his daughter. But someday, he was going to have to tell Gracie the whole truth, not just what he'd been placating her with these last two years. He was going to need to tell her that her mom wasn't coming back. That he really couldn't say if she'd ever loved them, because, let's be honest, who the hell would just walk out on their family like that?

He looked over at Gracie's preschool picture on the mantel. The one with the ridiculously wavy hair, because Isabel had taken her to her stylist for a "big girl blowout." Sam had never seen that picture. She'd never been around when Gracie had eaten that bag of Twix at Halloween, or had cried herself to sleep in those early days because she missed her mommy so much. Two years, but it felt like a lifetime of things Sam had missed. Of things she'd *chosen* to miss.

A familiar anger threatened to choke Ben where he stood. She'd never told him why she left, but their fights leading up to that moment had given him a pretty good idea. She'd resented him for wanting to settle down. And she resented Gracie for tying her down. There were probably other reasons, sure, but those were the hard-and-fast ones that he always came back to on nights like this when he felt especially alone, if not lonely.

He'd stopped trying to figure out if there'd been any signs that he'd missed, and had settled into this new reality. It had taken a while, but he and Gracie were okay. For now. As long as they had each other, they'd manage.

Rubbing the back of his neck, he headed down the hallway toward his daughter's room. No, he definitely wasn't ready to let another woman into his life. Someone he might end up loving. Or worse, that Gracie might end up loving.

Someone who might then turn around and leave them both.

Isabel might say life was too short for that kind of thinking. But Ben couldn't think of it any other way.

Chapter Four

"Is this Wednesday or Thursday?" Frances asked.

"It's Thursday." Kyla looked up from the cash register and watched Frances tap on the wall calendar with her index finger.

"I'm having lunch with Donna today. I'm glad I asked. I've been thinking it's Wednesday all morning."

Kyla's heart twisted. She'd reminded her only half an hour ago what day it was. Frances's memory seemed to be getting worse by the week. Although that probably had a lot to do with the fact that Kyla was here now, and witnessing it in person. Still, it worried her, and she knew she was going to have to call Stella and Marley soon. They needed to come up with some kind of plan moving forward. If things continued like this, Frances wouldn't be able to handle the house by herself, let alone the candy shop. And that meant there would eventually be hurdles for her to clear. Would she give the women she thought of as daughters the power to help her? Emotionally, as well as legally? They were questions that would need to be answered soon, for Frances's sake.

"I haven't seen Donna in forever," Kyla said, picturing Frances's very best friend, with the dyed red hair and penchant for swearing. They were quite a pair. "How is she?"

"Oh, you know Donna. Full of piss and vinegar."

Kyla laughed, letting her worries fall away for a moment. It was a beautiful morning. Main Street sparkled after last night's rain, and the sun shone in through the big front window, lighting everything up in gold. They'd just unlocked the front doors, but so far, the shop was empty. Peaceful and quiet after the relative chaos of their after-dinner rush last night. Kyla was glad. It was nice having this time alone with Frances.

Jacques stretched dramatically from his princess bed on the counter, looking like a chubby miniature lion.

Kyla gave him a scratch underneath the chin, and thought about Gracie coming in to see him the other day. She'd been so cute the way she'd made a beeline for the cat, leaving her poor father in her dust down the sidewalk.

At the thought of Ben, her chest tightened. *Good*

grief. She needed to get a handle on this before it got to her. Or he got to her. Whichever came first.

"It looks like it's going to be a pretty day," Frances said, putting her hands on her hips and staring out the window. The tourists were just starting to make their appearance—walking down the sidewalk and peering in the shop windows. Soon, there'd be a steady stream, and it would be lunchtime before they knew it.

"Not much wind," she continued, "which is nice. Sometimes I think it's going to blow me away up there at the house."

Kyla came out from behind the counter, and put her arm around the older woman. She was taller than Frances, but only by an inch or so. She could remember looking up at her as a little girl. Looking up *to* her. Frances had been her first real example of a strong, squared-away woman, which was something she came to aspire to. At the same time, that aspiration had made her feel guilty—disloyal to her mother, who had always struggled with everything in her life. Addiction, men, her self-worth. And most of all, it seemed, being a parent that her daughter could count on.

"I can remember it blowing so hard during storms, I thought the entire house would fall over," Kyla said. "And the power going out. Remember that? We all used to pile in your bed and tell ghost stories?"

Frances laughed. "You'd get so scared."

That had been right after her mother died. On her

worst nights, Kyla would imagine her own mom as a restless spirit, drifting over the old Victorian, looking for all the things that had eluded her on earth. It had taken a long time for that image to disappear, but the feeling had remained. And the question of whether or not her mother was finally at peace now, after a lifetime of sadness and despair. It was one of the reasons why Kyla had to leave Christmas Bay. The need to run from those questions, and from those lingering feelings of doubt, had been all-consuming. But they'd followed her anyway.

Even now, even all these years later, she couldn't help but wonder if she hadn't been taken from her mother when she had, if she would've been able to prevent the worst of it. Maybe. Maybe not. But the choice had been taken from her, too.

Swallowing the ache in her throat, she gave Frances another squeeze before wrapping her arms around herself, as if warding off a chill.

"There's Ben," Frances said.

Kyla looked up. "Where?"

"Driving by. See?"

Sure enough, there was his cruiser heading toward the police department, a bronzed arm waving outside the window. A woman on the sidewalk waved back.

Kyla pursed her lips, trying her best to ignore the fluttering of her heart. Ben Martinez was like a celebrity in Christmas Bay. Everyone knew him. Most everyone seemed to like him. This wasn't unlike high school, when he'd stepped onto the football field to a collective roar on Friday nights. Kyla had tried to block a lot of Ben out over the years, but these memories stubbornly remained. Mostly because as a kid, like everyone else, she had been in awe of him. Not just of the football player, but of the boy. Handsome, kind, on the verge of ruling the world. She'd been smitten. She'd been in love. At least, what she'd understood of love at the time.

Until he'd betrayed her.

The front door opened with a little tinkle of the bell, and Kyla looked over, shaken out of her memories. But when she saw Hunter Mohatt in his hoodie and threadbare sneakers, she felt her shoulders slump. *Uh-oh.* She really didn't feel like chasing him down the street again.

Taking a deep breath, she resisted the urge to tell him to leave. How would he learn if nobody ever gave him a chance? Even so, she steeled herself as he approached, ready to stop him in case he shoved something up his shirt. Then she really would press charges, and would feel more than justified doing it.

"Hi there, honey," Frances said. Completely unaware this was their shoplifter from the other day.

"Hi," Hunter mumbled, looking embarrassed.

Good, Kyla thought. *He should be embarrassed.* She was glad he was getting a good look at Frances today, seeing for himself how sweet she was. If Ben's lecture didn't get through, maybe something as simple as this would. He sure seemed uncomfortable. But that didn't necessarily mean anything. Maybe he was just hungry for some licorice, and had a crazy amount of gumption.

"I know you're probably not too excited to see me," he said to Kyla.

"I'm just surprised to see you," she said. "That's all."

He took an audible breath, and his gaze shifted to Frances, who was watching all this with a curious expression on her face.

"You two know each other?" she asked.

Hunter's cheeks colored. Kyla had only been in his presence twice, but blushing seemed to be an endearing quality of his. Although, it probably drove him bananas.

"I took your tip jar the other day," he said to Frances. "I just came back to say I'm sorry. It was dumb. It was just sitting there, and…" It wasn't any kind of excuse, but it appeared he already knew that. He blushed even deeper. "Anyway, I'm sorry."

Kyla's heart squeezed. He had this effect on her. Either he was being honest, and he really was sorry, or she was the worst kind of sucker.

"We all make mistakes," she said. "They're a part of life. The most important thing is to learn from them and move on."

He nodded.

"I've owned this shop a long time," Frances said, "and can honestly say you're the first person who's come in to apologize for taking something. We've gotten a few notes over the years, but never anyone in person. You've got guts, kid."

He shrugged. "I just felt bad."

"Well, we think you're very brave," Kyla said. She walked over to the jar of Tootsie Pops and took the lid off. "Have a Tootsie Pop. On us."

He was probably too old for such a sentiment, but she couldn't help it. He just looked so baby-faced today.

He smiled. "Thanks."

"I heard that Chief Martinez came to talk to you," she said. "He likes you."

Hunter unwrapped the Tootsie Pop and put it in his mouth. "He just doesn't want me getting in trouble anymore," he said around it.

"Well, no. But that doesn't mean he can't like you, too."

He took the sucker out with a smack. "My Dad was mad, but it would've been way worse if you'd pressed charges. He's got a bad temper."

Kyla didn't know what "way worse" meant, but she didn't really have to know the specifics. She remembered Ben telling her how rough his home life was.

"I don't know why he cares so much," Hunter mumbled. "He does worse stuff. At least I took the money for a reason."

Kyla's brows rose. A minute ago, it had been because the tip jar was just sitting there.

"And what was that?" Frances asked.

"My Mom's been needing some stuff around the

house. Stupid, but you know. That was like, what I was thinking at the time."

Kyla recognized the look on her foster mother's face as the words settled between them. Growing up, she'd seen it too many times to count. In fact, Frances had worn that look the night she'd picked Kyla up from children's services, and had taken her up to Cape Longing for the first time. It was a mixture of empathy and compassion. Of knowing exactly what you might be going through, even if you might not understand the enormity of it yourself. That look had a way of melting even the toughest of hearts. Kyla should know—it had eventually melted hers.

"What kinds of things does your mom need, honey?" Frances asked.

"Oh. Nothing. It's no big deal."

Kyla and Frances exchanged a glance.

"My Dad wouldn't like it if he knew I was here," Hunter continued, looking nervous all of a sudden. "He was pissed that Chief Martinez even came to talk to us. Pissed at you too, I think."

Kyla frowned. "Why me?"

"He probably blames you for the cops coming to our house in the first place. Even though it was my fault. My Dad doesn't need a ton of reasons to be pissed, though. He's mad pretty much all the time anyway."

Kyla didn't even know what to say to that. What she wanted to *do* was put an arm around his skinny shoulders, offer him some more candy and fix his crappy home life for him. But of course, she wasn't any fairy godmother, and this definitely wasn't some kind of small-town fairy tale. It was real life, and real life was messy and complicated, and sometimes you just had to stand there not knowing what to say.

"Here." Frances walked over to the counter. Then wrote something on a sticky note and handed it to Hunter. "This is my number. I want you to call if you ever need anything, okay? Even if it's just to talk."

An outsider watching this unfold might think Frances would make an unlikely ally for a fifteen-year-old boy. Her platinum-blond hair, her bedazzled sweatshirts, her penchant for calling people honey and sweetheart. But an outsider would also see what Hunter most likely did—that she was offering because she meant it. Not because she wanted to fill the void, but because she was a genuinely good person, with a big heart.

Kyla took an even breath. Who knew if Hunter would ever reach out? The odds weren't great. But there might come a time in his young life that proved too much for him to handle, and if that time came with that sticky note in his pocket…who knew?

"In the meantime," Frances said, "you come back and see us again, okay? You're always welcome here."

Hunter smiled, and Kyla had a moment of wondering if he was actually holding back tears. But before they could say anything more, he turned and walked out the door.

Frances put her hands on her hips and eyed him through the window—heading down the sidewalk, pulling his hood up as he went.

Kyla watched him too, and wondered if a caring adult had ever given her their phone number as a kid, if she would've used it. It was impossible to know.

She glanced over at Frances. "What was that you were saying about tough love?"

"Oh, you know. I'm getting soft in my old age."

The door opened again in a swoosh of salty sea air, and this time it was none other than Ben Martinez.

Kyla's belly dropped. This guy was everywhere.

"Well, look who's here!" Frances said. "What a nice surprise!" She walked over to give him a hug. Then stood on her tiptoes and kissed him on the cheek. It wasn't easy—he towered over her, but he bent obligingly down, as if used to having to do this on the regular.

He looked especially handsome this morning in his uniform and a pair of dark aviator sunglasses. And when Kyla realized she was staring, she cleared her throat and reached for the broom in the corner so she'd look appropriately busy.

Ben smiled, swiping the glasses off and tucking them in his uniform pocket. "I need to stop by more often. Greetings like that are hard to come by."

"We don't kiss all our customers," Frances said. "Only our favorites."

His gaze shifted briefly to Kyla and she felt her

cheeks warm. She'd never kissed a customer in her life, favorite or no, but his eyes were teasing just the same. And before she knew it, she was imagining what it would be like to kiss him. To wrap her arms around his trim waist, and feel his mouth on hers.

She had to turn away before he could read the look on her face.

"I was just heading back to the station," he said, "and ran into Hunter out there. He said he came by?"

Frances scratched Jacques behind the ears, and he began to purr. "He came in to apologize, if you can believe that. I told him he's the only one who's ever apologized in person for shoplifting. That was a first."

Ben nodded. "I'd like to say I'm surprised, but I'm really not. There's something about him. I think he's special."

"And he looks so sad," Frances said.

Kyla swept the broom over the floor half-heartedly. She thought he'd looked sad the day he took the tip jar. Today, he'd looked *beyond* sad. Like that weight on his shoulders was getting heavier. Harder to bear. Of course, it was impossible to know what kinds of things Hunter truly struggled with, and how much of those had to do with his family life, but Kyla had to wonder.

Ben put his hands in his pockets, and rocked back on his boots. "I picked his dad up the other night at The Pump House. He was threatening another patron. Pretty much par for the course."

Kyla frowned. The Pump House was a local bar. It didn't have any of the seaside ambiance that the other two bars in town had, and therefore wasn't as preferred by the tourists. It served mediocre beer, and lots of it. Kyla had always hated the place. It had been a favorite haunt of her mother's in those early days when Kyla was little and being left alone more and more.

She stopped sweeping, and looked down at the small pile of dust she'd gathered, suddenly overwhelmed by the memories. Most of them were confusing, volatile. Some, she couldn't even picture clearly, because she'd been so young. They came mostly in the form of feelings—chilly, or downright cold, like sitting in a drafty house without a sweater. But some of them were happy, and those were the ones that she clung to so fiercely. Those were the ones that demanded her loyalty to her mother, even after all her failings. And there had been plenty of those.

She felt Ben watching her. Felt the heaviness of his gaze all the way to her bones.

"Are you okay?"

She forced a smile. "Just thinking."

"You know, I've been thinking, too," Frances said. "Ben, you know Hunter better than we do. How do you think he'd do with a part-time job?"

"Frances…" Kyla began.

"Now, I know what you're going to say. Being able to trust him and all that. But it's not like he'd be here by himself. One of us would always be with him. We could start out with just a few hours on the weekends to see how it goes."

Ben looked over at Kyla and raised his brows. They both knew Frances didn't need anything else on her plate right now. Especially a teenage boy who was clearly in the midst of acting out, whatever his reasons might be.

This wasn't like Frances, who was usually so careful about things. But at the same time, it was exactly like her. It was like her usual shrewdness was being stripped away, leaving nothing but her tender heart underneath. Kyla wondered if this was what the memory loss would end up doing—make her as vulnerable as a child.

"I know you probably think this is crazy," Frances said, evenly. "But it's a way to help. We can make a difference here, and this town could use a little more of that, if I'm being honest."

It was hard to argue with that, since Kyla herself had been rescued by exactly this kind of logic.

Ben crossed his arms over his chest. "Normally, I'd try to talk you out of this, Frances. But I can see you're serious as a damn heart attack."

Her blue eyes sparkled.

"So, I'll just tell you to use your best judgment. Keep an eye on him, which I know you'd do anyway. And if you need me, I'll only be a few doors down."

Frances smiled. "Okay, then. We'll wait to see if he comes back. And if he does, I'll take that as a sign, and ask if he's interested. Who knows? Maybe he'll tell me to take a flying leap. But I don't think so. This would be a chance for him to make his own money. But mostly, it'd be a chance for him to get out of his house for a few hours at a time, and do something worthwhile." Her gaze settled on Kyla. "Do I have your blessing on this, honey?"

"You don't need my blessing. You know I'll support you, whatever you want to do."

After a few seconds, Ben clapped his hands together. "Well, ladies, I'd better get going. I've got a mountain of paperwork."

"Wait!" Frances opened one of the bins and stuffed some gummy worms into a little white bag. "Give these to our girl, okay?"

"You're going to spoil her."

"Yes, but all little girls need to be spoiled. It's the law."

"Is it?"

"You should know. You're the lawman around here."

Taking the bag, he winked and turned to go. And as he walked out the door, the sun on his broad shoulders, Kyla's stomach twisted. No matter how confident Frances was about offering Hunter a job, she was still uneasy about the possible fallout. She knew she wouldn't be able to relax until she made sure that Ben was okay with it too, and not just saying he was to be polite.

"Be right back, Frances."

"Where are you going?"

"I just want to thank Ben for watching out for things. With the shop and everything." That was true. But not the *whole* truth.

Frances seemed satisfied, though, and headed back behind the counter.

Pushing the door open, Kyla hurried after him.

"Ben!" she called. "Wait up!"

He turned, and smiled that smile. The one that sent shivers up her spine, in spite of everything.

"What's up?"

She pulled her sweater close. It would be a few hours before it really warmed up. She could hear the waves crashing against the beach in the distance, knowing how icy the water would be, even though it was summertime. That was the Oregon coast for you—beautiful, but colder than a polar bear's toenail. As Frances liked to put it.

"I know you're busy," she said, "but I just wanted to make sure you don't think this is the worst idea in the history of ideas?"

"What? The Hunter thing?"

She nodded.

"Honestly, I'm not worried about him," he said. "He's harmless. But I do worry about how much Frances should be taking on with this memory loss, though."

"So, you've noticed?"

He nodded. "Yeah."

"I know she seems pretty sure about things, and most of the time, I think she is. But other times…"

"Just remember," Ben said. "I'll be right here if you need me."

Kyla's chest warmed. It was hard not to be taken in by that. She couldn't deny there was a part of her that wanted to lean into it. Let him watch over her, just like that old song. But then she'd remind herself that she only needed his professional opinion, and that was it.

Someone called his name from across the street, and he turned to wave. He really was a Christmas Bay celebrity. There was a pink smear on his jaw, and she smiled as she recognized Frances's lipstick from her kiss earlier.

He turned back and caught her looking. "What?"

"Nothing. It's just that you've got something… right here." She touched her own cheek.

"Where?" He rubbed his fingers over the lipstick smudge, but it stayed put. He could thank Maybelline for that.

"Right…there."

Kyla stepped closer and pointed, but he wasn't getting it.

"What is it?" he asked.

"Just lipstick. From when Frances kissed you. Here…let me just…"

She reached up and rubbed her thumb over it. And the feel of his stubbled jaw sent a jolt of electricity through her core.

"There," she said, stepping quickly back. "Got it."

"Thanks. Couldn't have gone back to work like that. Too many wagging tongues around here."

That was the understatement of the century. Kyla guessed if he *had* gone back to the station with lipstick on his face, word would've spread by tonight that he was having some kind of sordid affair. That was just how small towns worked. Not a lot of room for privacy, but a ton of room for made-up stories.

"I'm guessing you might not have missed that about Christmas Bay," he said. "Not as many gossips in Portland?"

"There were probably just as many gossips, but people were just too busy to notice."

"Not here. You have dinner with someone, and boom. It's The Real Housewives of Jackson County."

She laughed. Then remembered why she'd chased him down in the first place. And it didn't have anything to do with his dinner plans.

"Okay," she said, clasping her hands together. "Well, thanks. I guess we'll just see what happens with Hunter."

He nodded as she took another step back. It seemed like she was always trying to tear herself away from Ben in one way or another. He was like a magnet that kept pulling her in, despite all her efforts to resist.

She remembered feeling that way as a girl, too. Even after he'd told the school counselor about her mom. Even after her anger at him threatened to swallow her whole. She'd still been drawn to him. To the thought of him, and even now, that scared her.

He watched her, his dark eyes revealing nothing. If Ben was drawn to anyone or anything, it didn't show on his handsome face. It was unnerving to be feeling this upside down, with him looking so relaxed and in control. She had to wonder if she made him feel anything at all.

"I'll be right here if you need me," he said again.

As if she'd forget.

Chapter Five

Kyla leaned against the sturdy iron railing of the widow's walk, and looked out over the ocean. It was blue-green tonight, almost tropical looking where the water was shallower near the coastline. The salty breeze whipped her hair across her face, and she brushed it away, breathing the sea air deep into her lungs.

She had a lot of favorite spots in Frances's old house. Favorite places to read, favorite places to be alone. But the widow's walk had always been her favorite place to think. To contemplate life. Or more specifically, *her* life, and how, like the ocean itself, it was constantly changing and adapting to the world around it. Sometimes for the better. But not always.

Sighing, she rested her elbows against the railing

and settled her chin in the palm of her hand. It would be dark soon. Sometimes, especially since returning to town, Kyla felt overwhelmed by her memories. Sometimes she felt stuck in her past, unable to accept the gift of a new day. Of being able to heal and move on. But then other times…

She licked her lips, tasting the salt there. She'd been gone from Christmas Bay for a long time, but she'd surprised herself with how fast she'd settled back into life here. What she and Ben had joked about earlier was true—it was a small town with small-town problems, gossip being only one of them. But it was also a part of her that Portland had never become. She was a small-town girl. She'd almost forgotten that about herself. Or maybe she'd wanted to forget that. But being back here, it was getting harder and harder to deny.

A flash of light caught her eye, and she looked down to see a car making its way up the gravel drive, its headlights cutting through the pines. She frowned. Frances had gone for a walk, so she was sure they weren't expecting anyone.

She pushed away from the railing, and headed down the curving staircase inside. Then looked out the sheer curtains in the living room, watching as a white BMW pulled into the driveway. Nobody she knew drove that kind of car.

With a tickle of nerves in her belly, she opened the front door and waited while whoever it was turned their engine off. It was dusk now, the evergreens next to the driveway casting a long shadow, but Kyla could make out a woman in the passenger seat. And that bouffant hair looked familiar. *Frances?*

Kyla squinted through the gritty light as the door opened. And sure enough…

Frances stepped out and waved. "Had a little bit of trouble, but it's alright! I ran into Isabel and she gave me a ride."

"Are you okay?" Kyla asked, rushing over. Their driveway was steep, and with the mist and fog, it could get slippery. But she seemed fine. Maybe a little too cheerful, which was usually her way of glossing things over.

"Fine, fine."

Taking a deep breath, Kyla looked over at the other woman climbing out of the car, and finally let herself process who it was. Isabel. Her best childhood friend…

She smiled slowly as the recognition set in. Of course, Isabel looked very different now. No longer the dark-haired little girl Kyla remembered, she'd grown into a lovely woman who was smiling back at her now. She'd never held any resentment toward Isabel. It was her own embarrassment and shame that had kept them apart all those years.

Without a word, she walked over to her friend and gave her a hug.

Isabel laughed into her hair. For Kyla, it was like the rest of the world fell away for a second, and she was ten years old again.

"It's so good to see you," she said, pulling away.

"It's good to see you, too."

"I'm sorry I never called…"

"Don't be silly, Kyla. We were kids."

"But I mean later," she said. "I should've called you later."

"Well, I could've called you, too. I guess I was too worried you'd hang up. But when Ben told me you were back here and working with Frances, I decided to make you some enchiladas and tamales. Your favorites. I knew you wouldn't be able to resist."

The warm, savory scent drifted from one of the car's cracked windows, making Kyla's mouth water. She could remember sitting down to dinner with the Martinez family on Sunday nights, so hungry the pains in her belly made her wince.

"You were right," she said. "I can't."

Frances headed toward the house, then called over her shoulder. "I'm going to put some tea on! You two can catch up inside."

Isabel frowned then, waiting as Frances closed the front door behind her. The lights flickered on in the kitchen, and somewhere close a bullfrog croaked through the trees.

Kyla shivered, but not because of the evening chill. It was because of the look on the other woman's face. The knowing tilt to her mouth.

"Frances said she was having trouble when you picked her up," she said. "What kind of trouble?"

Isabel looked over at the house and took a deep

breath. "She didn't want me to say anything. She doesn't want to worry you, but of course you need to know…"

"What?"

Isabel's gaze settled on Kyla again. "She was lost."

Kyla stared at her.

"I guess she tried a shortcut on her way back," Isabel continued quietly. "To be fair, it was through that new neighborhood on Grisham, and the road twists and turns, and then curves back around through the woods."

"Yes, but…" Kyla shook her head. Frances knew this area like the back of her hand. Even with the signs from the last few weeks, it was still hard to believe. Or maybe she didn't *want* to believe it, because that would mean her condition was more advanced than she thought.

"I know you're thinking the worst," Isabel said, "but it's going to be okay. She's going to be okay. Yes, there's definite evidence of decline, but these things don't happen overnight. It's gradual. And I know that probably doesn't make you feel any better, but it's a good thing to recognize it early. I've seen a lot of people so unwilling to accept it, that by the time things get worse, they're not prepared. Especially emotionally."

Kyla nodded. She knew that was true, but it didn't make it any easier. How were they going to negotiate this? Would they eventually need to hire someone to come to the house? Even though Kyla knew this was a realistic solution, and one that a lot of people had to resort to, the thought twisted her gut. No matter how vetted someone was, they'd still be a stranger. What if they took advantage of Frances? Or worse, mistreated her when she was at her most vulnerable?

She touched her temple, feeling a headache coming on.

"Hey."

She looked over at Isabel.

"It's going to be okay," her friend repeated. "She was lost, but she snapped out of it pretty fast when I pointed out the pathway to her. And Frances has an entire town of people who love and care about her. It takes a village, right?"

Kyla smiled weakly. They liked to say that in the foster system a lot. And while it was true that people should watch out for each other, Kyla knew that wasn't always the case. They got busy with their own lives and their own problems. But she wasn't going to voice any of this to Isabel, who was only trying to make her feel better.

"Do you have time to come inside?" she asked. "Frances probably has a whole spread out by now. She made cookies last night, and there's banana bread in the fridge."

"I'd love to. And let's not forget your dinner."

Isabel opened the BMW's back door, and grabbed a casserole dish which she handed over to Kyla. It was still warm.

"The best enchiladas in three counties," Kyla said

dreamily. "I'll be working them off for a week, but totally worth it."

"Ahh," Isabel said as they headed toward the front door. "Ben said he saw you at the gym the other day."

So, he'd mentioned that... She really shouldn't care if he talked about her at all, but her stupid heart fluttered anyway.

They stepped inside the foyer and Kyla closed the door behind them. It smelled like a bakery, and she knew she'd been right about the banana bread. Frances was going all out.

Isabel looked around. "Wow. This place is incredible."

Kyla looked around too, trying to see it through Isabel's eyes. To her friend, it was a well-known landmark. A breathtaking piece of architecture that was visible from certain parts of town—teetering on the edge of the cliffs with its spectacular view of the ocean. It had such a history, some people in Christmas Bay even thought it was haunted. She got it. That was romantic. And the house fit the part, with Frances giving it a spooky makeover for the trick or treaters every Halloween.

Inside, the dark cherrywood staircase curved gracefully toward the second and third floors like a dancer, and was the first thing you saw when you walked through the door. At Christmastime, Frances wrapped twinkle lights and a fresh garland around the banister, making the entire house smell like pine.

To the right, was a huge sitting room with floor-to-ceiling bookcases, and bay windows that over-looked the yard and the blustery sea beyond. Antique lamps filled the space with warm yellow light, making the original hardwood floors gleam. And then there was the kitchen—completely remodeled, but reflecting the Victorian era of the house beautifully. Frances said it was her favorite room. But to be honest, every room was her favorite. The house was her baby. Plain and simple. But to Kyla, it was her first real home.

"It must be getting a lot for Frances to take care of," Isabel said with a frown. "That yard alone…"

"It's a lot. I worry. Those rosebushes have a life of their own, believe me."

"Girls," Frances called from the kitchen. "Tea's on!"

Kyla smiled. It felt like they were in the sixth grade again—bonding over the Backstreet Boys and watching VH1 in Isabel's bedroom. There must've been a hundred times that they'd been called for meals just like this. "Girls! Dinner!"

They walked into the kitchen where Frances had three steaming cups of tea waiting on the table. The banana bread was waiting too—warm, with butter seeping into the thickly cut slices.

"Here, honey. Let me take that."

Frances took the casserole dish from Kyla and motioned for everyone to sit. She'd brought out her best china, delicate porcelain with a delicate cherry blossom pattern that Kyla had only seen a handful of times.

This visit from Isabel must be special. Or maybe she knew it was special to Kyla.

Isabel took a sip of her tea. "Oh, this is delicious. What kind?"

"Vanilla chai. Kyla's favorite."

"It is my favorite. And I haven't had any since the last time I was home. Thanks for all this, Frances."

"Of course. I'm just happy you girls found your way back to each other again. I know how close you used to be."

"Kyla…" Isabel set her tea down, cupping it in her hands. She stared at it for a few seconds, before looking back up again. "I feel like I need to apologize."

Kyla put her tea down, too. "For what?"

"For what happened when we were kids. For how you were taken from your house."

It had been a taboo subject for so long, Kyla hadn't had to acknowledge it until just now. Even Ben, whom she'd been dancing around since she got home, hadn't tried talking about it directly. At least not in a way that made her feel like he expected a response.

Isabel, on the other hand, would be a different story. She was clearly just as gutsy as she used to be. Just as bold.

Kyla ran her thumb over the rim of the teacup. It had a tiny chip that caught her skin. Making her think of the dishes in her cupboard when she was little. They'd all been broken in one way or another. Just like her heart.

"You don't have to apologize, Isabel," she said. "It wasn't your fault."

"I know that now. But back then I had a hard time with it."

"It was a long time ago."

Isabel reached out and put her hand over Kyla's. "Being taken away like that changed your whole life, and I'm just sorry that I wasn't there for you."

"When I look back, I realize that if I'd let you in, you would've been there for me. I was just so confused, that I didn't…" She couldn't finish that sentence, because she really didn't know what she was trying to say. She didn't what? The truth was, she was still confused.

"I know," Isabel said. "You were mad at Ben. You felt like he betrayed you."

Swallowing the sudden lump in her throat, Kyla looked past Frances and out the darkened window. The moon was almost full tonight. A huge silver globe in the night sky, dwarfing the stars twinkling around it.

"The truth was, my mom wasn't taking care of me," she managed. "She tried. In her own way, I know she tried. But she just wasn't, and I get that."

"And just because she wasn't taking care of you like she should've been, that doesn't mean you didn't love her. And that she didn't love you."

Kyla looked back at Isabel through blurry eyes. *This.* Exactly this. So many of the friends she'd made later on hadn't understood her childhood. When she'd confided to a precious few what had happened with her mother, they couldn't get why she'd cared so much about her. *But she hurt you*, they'd say. *Thank God you were taken away when you were. Otherwise, who knows what might've happened?*

Kyla had heard it all. And each one of those words had made her feel like the fierce love she'd had for her mom was misplaced. Like it was wasted, or not earned. They made her feel wrong for loving her like she had. Like she still did.

So, confused? Yeah. She was confused, and then some.

"Ben just cared about you so much," Isabel continued softly. "We all did. I'm just sorry it happened the way it did, and…"

She didn't have to finish that sentence. Kyla knew what she wanted to say. That her mother had accidentally overdosed before Kyla ever had the chance to make peace with any of it. And that's where the anger at Ben came in. Misplaced? Probably. But it was what it was.

"You know," she said, wanting to shift the subject toward something lighter. Isabel looked like she was on the verge of tears. "My mom was a hot mess, but there were good times, too. Every year she made sure to stay clean for my birthday, remember that? The parties were epic. I know she was trying to make up for everything else, but those parties, though."

Isabel smiled. "Oh, I remember. She was a great baker. I was always jealous of your cakes."

"Everybody was. Kids came to my parties who didn't even like me. They just came for the food."

"You never told me that," Frances said. "That your mom liked to bake."

Kyla nodded. There were still things she didn't talk about, even with Frances. Sometimes even the good memories could be painful, slicing through her heart like a knife. She really didn't know if it would ever get any easier.

"Speaking of birthdays," Isabel said, "my oldest has one on Saturday."

"Joe?" Frances asked. "How old?"

"Seven. He wants a puppy, which isn't going to happen. But we *are* doing a beach birthday party if the weather cooperates. And we're getting him a bike, so there's that."

Kyla smiled, leaning her elbows on the table. "How many kids do you have, Isabel?"

"Two. Two *very* rambunctious boys."

"I bet they keep you on your toes."

"Well, they keep my husband on his toes. He works from home, so he gets to do a lot of the wrangling."

"And you're a nurse-practitioner?"

Isabel nodded.

"Your parents must be proud. I know they were hoping you'd go into healthcare."

"Well, I was obsessed, remember? I was always trying to nurse everyone growing up—my dolls, my brothers and sisters. Now at least I get paid for it, so that's a plus."

"I can't believe you made time to come over here with dinner," Kyla said. "You must be so busy."

"I am, but I'm lucky I have help. Jason's great. So is Ben. He's a single dad, so I try to help him as much as I can, too. It's hard, but he makes it work."

Kyla opened her mouth to say something, then closed it again.

"What?" Isabel asked.

"Nothing."

"It's something. I can tell by the look on your face."

"What look?"

"That one. The one that says you don't care, but you really do."

Kyla felt her cheeks warm. Some things never changed. Isabel still knew her better than most of her friends knew her now. It was sweet. And disconcerting. She'd never been able to lie to Isabel Martinez.

"Okay," she said. "I was just going to ask why Ben is…"

She told herself that despite what Isabel thought, she was just curious about Ben and his story. When it came right down to it, she didn't *really* care. And she guessed if she repeated it enough, she might actually start believing it.

"Single?" Isabel finished with a smile.

Kyla looked down at her teacup and shrugged.

"His ex-wife just walked out one day," Isabel said. "I've tried to wrap my brain around it, but I'll be honest—it's hard. I know marriages are complicated, and people have legitimate problems that keep them from being happy. But Gracie…"

Kyla looked up at the sound of Isabel's voice. It had turned sharp, unforgiving.

"She's so innocent. She doesn't understand any of this. What I don't get, is how could anyone leave their own child?"

It was a tough question, and one that hit closer to home than Kyla would've liked. Her mother never went anywhere. Physically, at least. But she'd left a long time before Kyla was ever taken away.

Isabel must've noticed her expression, because she immediately frowned. "Oh, I'm sorry, Kyla. I didn't mean anything by that."

"Please. It's fine."

"Anyway," Isabel said. "She told Ben she was done, and nobody has heard from her since. At least, her family isn't admitting to hearing from her, but she's estranged from them, so I don't know that she would've kept in touch anyway."

"How long were they together?"

"Long enough to screw him up."

Kyla frowned. She wouldn't wish that on anyone. She knew what it was like to be damaged. People could see it from a mile away.

"I'm sorry," she said. "He didn't deserve that."

"No, he didn't. But that's life, I guess." Isabel smiled. "I'm just happy you're back. Let's focus on that."

"Deal."

"You know, we'd love for you and Frances to come to Joe's birthday party. Most of the family is going to be there, and they'd be so happy to see you. Mom was asking about you just the other day."

Kyla had always had a soft spot for Carla Martinez, and knew the feeling was mutual. But this was opening a door she wasn't sure she wanted to walk through yet. If at all.

"Please?" Isabel said, clasping her hands in front of her chin. "I know it's been a minute, and our family is big and loud and overwhelming, but we've missed you, Kyla Bear. Will you come?"

And that did it. Hearing Isabel use her childhood nickname melted her heart.

She laughed, unable to help it. "You're not going to make this easy, are you?"

"How'd you know?"

"Lucky guess."

"And what does Joe want for his birthday?" Frances asked. "I've been wanting to check out that new toy store on Fourth Street, and now I have an excuse."

"Honestly, Frances, just bring him a bag of gummy worms and he'll be thrilled. He has the same addiction as Gracie, unfortunately."

Kyla's stomach dipped. Of course Gracie would be there, probably with her dad. But for some reason, the thought hadn't fully formed until just now.

"This Saturday at Harris Beach," Isabel said.

"One o'clock. And come hungry, because there will be tons of food."

"We'll be there," Kyla said, already wondering what to wear.

Chapter Six

Ben helped Gracie out of the truck, where her pink tutu was immediately snatched up by the wind. It blew right over her head. Thank God he'd insisted on her wearing shorts underneath.

She yanked it back down again, unfazed. She looked so cute, so supremely *six*, that Ben's heart caught in his throat. She was growing up so fast. Before he knew it, she'd be filling out college applications and going to her senior prom. But Isabel would tell him to relax, to slow down. Not to miss out on today because of thoughts of losing her to adulthood tomorrow. And she'd be absolutely right.

She tucked her hand in his, and it reminded him of a little paw. His little cub, so adventurous and unafraid. Even though she'd experienced more hurt than any child should at her age, Gracie was a force to be reckoned with. Tutu and all.

She tugged on his hand and he lengthened his strides to keep up.

"Ooohh! They're flying a kite!"

He looked down the beach, and sure enough, a colorful dragon kite dipped and bobbed on the breeze. The ocean was subdued today, sparkling turquoise underneath the summer sun. Noisy seagulls flew overhead, their wings speckled gray against the robin's-egg sky. It was a perfect afternoon for a party.

"Do you think we'll have cake before or after presents?" Gracie asked.

"I'm not sure. Nana made lunch, though, so no cake until you eat something good for you."

"Quesadillas?"

"Maybe."

"Nana knows not to put chicken in mine." She made a face. "Yuck."

"Gracie…"

"I know. Be grateful for what we have."

"That's right. Even when it's chicken."

"Even when it's chicken." She sighed dramatically.

"Look, honey, there's Joe."

"Can I go now?"

"Yes, but be careful of those rocks. And stay where I can see you. And do *not* go near that water, understand?"

She nodded, but kept watching her cousins playing tag on the beach.

"Gracie," Ben said, waiting until she looked up at him. "Do you understand?"

"Yes, Daddy."

"Okay, then."

"Love you!"

Without another word, she let go of his hand and sprinted in the direction of the other kids, nothing but a streak of pink tulle in the wind.

Clutching Joe's present underneath his arm, Ben watched her go. Then shifted his gaze to the adults milling around the group of picnic tables at the edge of the beach. His dad was standing at the barbecue, where smoke curled into the air. He was wearing a flowered apron, and a Portland Trail Blazers cap turned backward. Ben's mom stood next to him, talking over his shoulder. Back-seat grilling, no doubt.

His brothers and sisters were all here with their families, along with a few miscellaneous friends. It was a typical Martinez birthday party. His family never missed an opportunity to gather. And eat.

Ben smiled, taking a step toward them. But stopped when he saw Frances talking with Isabel off to the side. If Frances was here…

Isabel hadn't mentioned inviting Kyla. But then again, she wouldn't have to. This was their party, not his. Still, there was a momentary prickle of irritation at his little sister. Sure, she wanted to reconnect with her old friend. But he also knew her well enough to guess there was another motive, too.

As if reading his mind, Isabel glanced over and waved sheepishly. Yeah. *Definitely* busted.

Gritting his teeth, he waved back.

"Your nephew is adorable."

Ben startled and turned at the sound of the voice behind him. And there she was. Looking beautiful in an army-green tank top and faded jeans. Her dark hair was up today—in a simple ponytail with silky tendrils blowing around her face.

Ben felt himself warm at the sight of her.

"I didn't know you were coming," he said.

"I didn't either. Until the other night when Isabel showed up with tamales and enchiladas. Which, by the way, were the best things I've ever eaten in my life."

"Better than Mom's?"

"Possibly. And I'll deny saying that, just so you know."

He glanced over at the barbecue. It didn't look like the food was anywhere near ready yet, and Isabel was now settled in a lawn chair, wearing a wide-brimmed hat and watching the kids play.

He turned back to her. "It looks like lunch might be a while. What do you say to a walk on the beach?"

The words were out and hanging there before he realized what he'd said. He waited, half expecting her to recoil at the suggestion.

"Actually," she said, "I'd like that. I didn't make it to the gym this morning, so this will help me get my steps in."

He smiled. "And the beach is better than the tread-mill from hell?"

"Also that."

"Just let me put Joe's present back in the truck, and we can head up toward the pier. The views there are pretty amazing. But you know that already."

The pier had been one of Kyla and Isabel's favorite hangouts as kids. Even though Isabel hadn't been allowed to go there without an adult, they'd snuck over there often anyway. Ben knew they'd go after school to feed the sea lions that sunned themselves on the planks below, and he'd told them he'd keep their secret as long as they stayed together and didn't talk to strangers. But Isabel had almost fallen in one day, and that was the end of that. She could've been killed.

That was around the time he'd learned that keeping someone's secrets was sometimes the worst thing you could do for them.

They headed down to the beach, stepping carefully over the rocks, and crossing a small stream snaking its way through the sand. Kyla wobbled a little, and Ben reached out to steady her before her sneakers got soaked.

Putting his hands in his pockets again, he looked out over the ocean as they made their way down the beach, with the foamy waves breaking only a few yards away. Salty spray hung in the air, clinging to his skin and making him wonder if Kyla was cold.

She was quiet, walking beside him with her arms crossed over her chest.

"Here," he said. "Let me switch sides." He stepped around her so he was closest to the water, hoping to shield her from the wind.

"Oh. Well, that was chivalrous of you."

"I live to serve."

"Actually, you literally *do* live to serve."

He thought about that for a second. "I guess I do. Protect and serve, that is. But I do it for a paycheck, so…"

"I'm guessing you'd do it even if you didn't get paid. You're kind of a natural at it."

"You think so?"

"The way you are with Hunter? You're a really good police officer, Ben."

It might've been more than she'd meant to say, because she looked down then and scuffed at the sand with the toe of her shoe.

They continued walking, but the silence between them felt more meaningful this time around. Like there were things to say, but neither one of them knew quite where to start.

Ben slowed, the cool breeze buffeting the back of his neck. The smell of the salt water tangy in his nose. And the woman beside him waking up memories inside him that had been sleeping for a long time. It was enough to make him glance over at her now. She wasn't a girl anymore. She was a grown woman, strong as steel. Yet she'd let down enough of her amor to show the slightest trace of tenderness around her edges. It accented her, like lace. He *still* wanted to protect her. Even all these years later.

He stopped then, hands still in his pockets, and turned to her. She stopped, too. Her eyes were almost lavender today. Next to the ocean, or simply what she wore, they seemed to change color. She was a chameleon.

"What?" she asked, reaching up to push a strand of hair away from her face.

He frowned. This walk had seemed like a good idea ten minutes ago. With his family milling about, and lunch about to be ready. But here, now, he wasn't so sure. He was so damn drawn to her, and he really didn't understand where that was coming from. Yes, she was gorgeous. But her looks alone weren't enough to justify the steady pounding of his heart as he stood there taking her in.

"We've never talked, Kyla," he said. "About you getting taken from your mom. I've always wanted to explain what happened. Why I did what I did."

She swallowed visibly. "I know why. I was being neglected. I understand."

"But you still blame me."

"It's complicated."

"I know it is. And I know how painful it was for you."

She looked away.

"Kyla…"

Slowly, she looked back. Her eyes were glassy.

"We weren't going to get involved," he said. "At least not until we knew for sure what was going on. That's what my parents said when I came to them about it. They didn't want you traumatized any more than you already were, and they thought as long as you were over at our place so much, we could keep an eye on you. But I was at school one day, and I'd said something before I even knew what I'd done. I'm not sorry about talking to that counselor, because you were suffering. That was obvious. But I can't tell you how sorry I am that your mom passed after that. I'm so sorry you didn't get to go home again."

Her chin was trembling now, but he could tell she was fighting it. He longed to pull her into his arms and hold her against his chest. He understood how it felt to be let down by someone who was supposed to love you. He understood how it felt to be alone.

Instead, he dug his hands farther into his pockets, just so he wouldn't be tempted to reach for her. Kyla had always had a hold on his heart. When she was little, he felt compelled to look out for her. Now she stood before him, grown, self-assured in a way that was both unfamiliar and wholly attractive, he felt compelled to ease her pain. In any way possible.

"I'm not usually this fragile," she said. "I'm not sure why now."

"Maybe it's a good thing. Talking about it."

It was absurd, really. Him giving anyone advice on how to deal with their emotions. He, who hadn't managed to let go of any of the anger that had been brewing inside him since the day Sam had walked out the door.

"I feel guilty," she said. "And as an adult, I know that doesn't make any sense. But I still feel guilty that I wasn't there to save her. If I'd been there, maybe… maybe…"

Her voice hitched. And that did it.

It didn't matter that they barely knew each other anymore. In this moment, it didn't matter that for the last few weeks he was sure she'd hated him. And he didn't care that Isabel was probably watching from down the beach at this point. He just wanted to comfort her, to make the burden she carried lighter, if he could.

He owed her that, at least.

Stepping forward, he did what he'd longed to do since that first day he'd seen her outside the candy shop. Breathing hard after chasing Hunter, her cheeks pink, her eyes compassionate despite everything, a feeling had welled up in his chest. At the time, he'd buried it—he'd had no business feeling such things for Kyla Beckett. Ever.

But now…now, he pulled her gently to him.

To his surprise, she rested her head against his chest, relaxing into him in a way he wouldn't have thought possible a minute ago. He felt her soft exhalation of breath into his shirt. It was warm, and painfully sweet.

He didn't say anything. Instead, he wrapped his arms around her and held her close. The wind blew strands of her hair across his face, bringing with it the smell of her shampoo. He hadn't planned this. He'd never meant to touch her at all. But that was the thing about Kyla. Everything about her was turning out to be a surprise.

After a minute, she sniffed and pulled away.

"This is embarrassing," she said, looking down. "I think I'm alright now. Sorry."

"Don't be ridiculous. We were practically family once, remember?"

"A long time ago."

"That doesn't mean we can't be friends again."

"I don't know, Ben. You don't know me anymore. I'm a hard person to be friends with."

"Why?"

She licked her lips. "You know, brick walls. I don't like to get hurt. That kind of thing. Cliché, but true."

"So, it'd be a one-sided friendship."

"Something like that."

He shrugged. "I can live with it. If you end up forgiving me, I can live with it."

"I forgive you."

He put his hands back in his pockets and watched as she picked up a small flat rock and threw it into the water. Four skips. He was impressed.

"Nice try," he said. "But I can tell when someone is blowing smoke."

She looked over at him.

"Police officer, remember?"

"Right."

"Saying you forgive me isn't the same thing as actually forgiving me."

She nodded, worrying her bottom lip with her teeth for a minute. "You're right," she finally said. "I think I just need time to work through things. I didn't think that being back in Christmas Bay would affect me like it has. But it's like no time has passed at all. It's just hard, that's all."

Judging by the look on her face, he knew the word *hard* didn't cut it. Not by a long shot.

"I'm still so mad," she continued, "that sometimes I'm afraid it's going to eat up what's left of me. Do you ever feel that way?"

He couldn't say he knew exactly how she felt, because he'd always had two loving parents. But he knew the part about feeling consumed by anger from Sam. It had become a cornerstone of his psyche. It did things to you.

"Yes," he said. "I do."

"And sometimes I don't know who I want to hate, and who to let off the hook. I don't want to hate my mom for what she did to me. I loved her. I still love my mom. It's easier to blame other people." She sighed. "I guess it sounds complicated."

His heart twisted at that. "It makes sense," he said quietly.

"You're a convenient punching bag."

"I get that, too."

"And I'd be lying if I said I trusted you completely."

"It's like we're the same person."

She laughed. And it sounded good to his ears. What happened with Kyla had always bothered him. And now that she was working right down the street from the station, he also knew he'd be seeing a lot of her this summer. It just made sense to try and fix this between them.

They stood there watching each other, not saying anything, until they heard their names being called from down the beach.

They turned at the same time to see Isabel with her hands cupped around her mouth. "Food is ready!"

Ben waved back. Then turned back to Kyla. "Food. I hope you're hungry."

"For your mom's cooking? I'm starving."

"Copy that. Let's go."

She stepped past him, and he let his gaze fall to the curve of her back. He swallowed hard. It looked like holding her in his arms, even for a minute or two, was going to have some consequences.

"Have a nice day!"

Frances held the door open as the elderly man shuffled past and out onto the sidewalk.

Kyla stood at the window, watching him go. He slapped his cane in front of him, and tipped his hat to a woman walking by. He'd come in to get candy for his grandson who would be visiting from Ohio this week. Naturally, Frances had led him straight to the gummy worms.

"Whew," Frances sighed, leaning down to give Jacques a pat. "It's been a circus today."

Kyla nodded. Mondays were usually slow. But not this one. She and Frances had been hopping since opening the doors that morning, but it looked like they were in for an after-lunch lull. Kyla was glad. She'd been distracted, off. And knew exactly why.

Walking around to the cash register, she wiped at some dust on the old-fashioned keys. Then straightened a bobblehead figurine of Elvis that Stella had sent a few days ago from Graceland. She was an Elvis fanatic.

"Feel like talking about it?" Frances asked.

She glanced up, hoping she looked appropriately clueless. "Talk about what?"

But Frances knew her too well. And besides, she'd seen her take a walk with Ben at the party. She'd probably seen them hugging, too. Everyone at the party had probably seen them hugging.

However, Frances was also good at giving her space, and not pushing when other mothers might want to. She knew Kyla had a tendency to retreat back into herself when things got complicated, and the subject of Ben Martinez was just that.

"You know what," Frances said evenly. "But if you'd rather not go there, I'll leave it alone."

"There's really nothing to talk about." Kyla shrugged, feeling her pulse tap traitorously behind her ears. "He just wanted to talk about my mom, that kind of thing. I haven't really thought too much about it."

Wow. What a whopper.

Frances stared at her, obviously not buying a word of that.

"Okay," she said. "Maybe I've been thinking about it a *little*."

"Uh-huh."

The truth was, she hadn't been able to stop thinking about it. How he'd pulled her close on the beach that day. How his embrace had given her shelter from the breeze—and the comfort she'd been so desperately seeking for so long. How the steady beat of his heart had felt, strong and sure next to her cheek. How clean his shirt had smelled, and the musky scent of his skin.

Looking away, she hoped Frances wouldn't recognize the expression on her face. Longing. Maybe even lust. She'd tried so hard to resist those feelings, but it turned out that resisting had only made them burn brighter, and with an intensity that scared her. Now she just had to figure out how she was going to smother this attraction to Ben once and for all. Until the summer was over and she went back to…

She frowned. Until she went back to where? It had been easy to forget these last few weeks, but this move to Christmas Bay was never supposed to be permanent. She was going to have to start thinking about her future soon. She knew of several places that were hiring in Eugene, and if worse came to worst, she could always sub until she found the right position.

"I just wish he wasn't such a nice guy," she said. "It'd be easier to hate him that way."

"You never hated him, honey. You *tried* to hate him. What you were was angry. And very hurt. Which was understandable, given the circumstances."

"I don't know anymore. I really don't."

"What else did he say?"

"That he was sorry," Kyla said, looking over at Frances. "I think he feels like he owes me something."

"Or maybe he just wants your forgiveness. In your heart, you're still angry. Aren't you?"

"That's what he said." Kyla sighed. "I guess I am."

"Sweetheart…"

Frances came over and rubbed a few circles on her back, something she always used to do when Kyla was upset. "It's going to be okay, you know. Being back here is hard—I know that. But I also think it's going to be therapeutic for you. Facing these things isn't easy, but it's a way forward."

"I'd love to believe that."

"There's no reason why you can't."

Kyla looked out the window to the tourists strolling by. It didn't seem like they had a care in the world, but of course that wasn't true. They were on vacation, some of them just for the day, but that didn't mean that their pain, their problems weren't waiting when they got home.

In some ways, she felt like she was on vacation in Christmas Bay, too. Like she was pushing everything off to the side, but knew eventually she'd have to face it. She thought about Frances getting lost the other night, and how hard the future might be for their little family.

"Frances," she said. "Have you thought about what you're going to do in a few years? With the shop, with the house…"

Frances frowned at that, and Kyla noticed some soft new wrinkles near the corners of her mouth. "Sometimes," she said. "But I don't like to. I don't want anything to change."

"But it's going to. You know that, right? Things always change eventually."

"Not if I fight them hard enough."

Kyla felt her stomach curl into itself. Just how was she going to negotiate this with someone she loved so much?

"Why?" Frances asked, sounding wary.

"I don't know. I'm a little worried, I guess."

"Well, you don't have to be. I'm fine. I mean, my memory isn't what it used to be, but whose is?"

Kyla steeled herself. She could tiptoe around this, but that would be a disservice to Frances, who'd always admired honesty above all else.

"Frances," she said slowly. "I think your memory is getting worse."

Her foster mother stiffened at that.

"And I do worry," Kyla said, plunging ahead, "because I love you, and I want what's best for you, and I'm not sure that juggling the house and the shop is going to be doable forever."

"Well, not forever, no. But as of right now, I'm fine, Kyla."

Pulling at a loose string on her sweatshirt, Kyla took a steadying breath. "Isabel told me what happened the other night."

"Oh, that. It wasn't a big thing. That neighborhood is new and confusing. You've said so yourself."

"I know. That's true. But what if she hadn't driven by when she had?"

"I would've eventually found my way home. Christmas Bay isn't that big. Honestly, honey, I think you're making too big a deal out of this."

But the way she said it, the way her chin was trembling, just slightly, told Kyla she was worried, too.

Kyla reached for her hand. "You know I'm here. We're all here for you."

"You have your own life. Stella and Marley have their own lives. I don't ever want to be a burden to any of you."

"You'd never be a burden. We're family."

It was the truth. What would she ever do without Frances? After all, Frances had become the anchor in Kyla's life when she needed one most. The thought of losing her, or her sharp, witty, intelligent mind, was simply too much to bear.

The door opened with a tinkle of the bell, and they both looked up at the same time.

There, in his signature hoodie and Converse All Stars, was Hunter. And when he saw them, he smiled wide.

"I just came in to say hey," he said. "And, you know. To get another Tootsie Pop." He jingled some change in his pocket. "Don't worry—I'm paying this time."

Frances looked over at her and raised her brows.

He looked from Kyla to Frances, and back again. "What?" he said.

Kyla laughed at the expression on his face. "Nothing," she said. "We were just hoping you'd be back in, that's all."

"Oh, yeah?"

"We absolutely were," Frances said. "I have a proposal for you."

"What kind of proposal?"

"An employment proposal, if you will."

Hunter frowned. "Am I in trouble?"

"No, honey. In fact, it's just the opposite. We want to offer you a job."

He stared at her. "A job... Why?"

"Because I think you have the potential to be very good behind the counter. You obviously know your candy." She winked. "But we'd have to start out slow, only a few hours on the weekends to see if it works out. To see how seriously you'd take it."

He seemed to be processing this, his blond hair falling over one eye. He was a cute kid. But Kyla still wondered how good an idea this really was. It could end up being great, or it could end up being a disaster. Only time, and Hunter himself, would tell.

"What do you think, hon?" Frances asked. "You can absolutely say no. We just thought we'd ask."

A smile crept over his mouth. "No, I want to."

"Alright then. You'd have to get your parents' permission, though."

Kyla watched him. "You said your dad was upset with me the other day. Do you think they'll be okay with this?"

"I'll make sure. And you said it would be on the weekends?"

"On the weekends to start," Frances said.

"Okay. I'll ask my mom tonight. I'm still confused, though. Why me?"

"Because you're a good kid, we can tell," Frances said. "And you might be a misunderstood kid because of the choices you've made lately. And sometimes it just takes some pride and responsibility to make a difference."

Kyla smiled at that. She'd been given the same speech when she was his age. She'd never gotten herself into any trouble, but Frances had clearly seen that she was sliding into a dark place where she couldn't be reached. So, she was offered a weekend job in the candy shop, too. And Frances was right. It had made all the difference.

"And bonus?" Kyla said. "All the Tootsie Pops you can eat."

Hunter laughed, clearly encouraged by this.

"There's one thing, though," Frances said. "You'll have to get your parents' permission, okay?"

Looking confused, Hunter glanced at Kyla.

Her heart sank. She so wished that she could protect Frances from the cruelty of this memory loss. But that wasn't how life worked. She couldn't protect her. But she could love her through it.

She reached out and touched Hunter's elbow. "It's such a nice day, and I have to walk down to the pharmacy for a few things. Why don't you walk with me, and I'll give you a rundown about the shop and the kinds of things you might be doing here. If you have a few minutes?"

He nodded. "Sure." Then turned to Frances. "'Bye."

"'Bye, honey."

Kyla followed him out the door and into the bright, sunny afternoon where the sea air felt like a caress against her skin. She put her hands in her jean pockets and turned to Hunter who was already watching her in anticipation. If he was going to work at Coastal Sweets, there were things he needed to know about

Frances. Things that would teach him much more than simply working in a candy shop could.

She smiled at him, wanting this to work out. For him. For all of them.

"How much do you know about dementia?" she asked.

Chapter Seven

"You said I could invite anyone I want!"

Gracie sat back in her booster seat in a huff. She scowled at Ben's reflection in the rearview mirror, and he had to work not to laugh. She was adorable when she got mad. However, right now she was acting out, and he didn't want to encourage that kind of behavior.

"I meant one of your friends from school. I *meant* a playdate."

Looking both ways at the stop sign, he eased on the gas again. This was the kind of thing he worried about. She was an only child, and spent so much time with him at the damn police station, she was starting to want to hang out with adults more than kids her own age.

"It *is* a playdate, and I want to have a playdate with Kyla!" She kicked the back seat.

"Hey," he growled. "Knock it off, young lady."

Her eyes immediately filled with tears. She was exhausted. They both were. She'd had a nightmare at four that morning. Which meant The Wiggles and Goldfish crackers until they'd both finally dozed off in front of the TV, and he'd gotten up for work after only a few hours of sleep—and a whole lot of worry.

He felt like he was blinking through sandpaper, and wasn't looking forward to his meeting at the city hall in half an hour. He was going to have to pretend to be awake while the mayor droned on and on about the Huckleberry Festival this fall.

He glanced at her again in the mirror. Then sighed and pulled his truck over to the curb. Tabitha was expecting them, but five minutes wouldn't make a difference.

He put the truck in Park, unbuckled his seat belt and twisted around to face her.

"Hey."

She sniffed, but didn't answer.

"Look at me, pumpkin."

After a few seconds, she did. Her eyes were red rimmed, her dark lashes spiked with tears.

"I know you want to invite Kyla over this weekend, and I know you like her a whole lot. I do, too. But she might not think it was just a playdate. She might think it was something else."

Gracie frowned. "Like what?"

"Like… I don't know. She might think it was me who was really inviting her over."

"Why?"

"Because she's a little old for playdates."

"She's not old like Frances."

He smiled a little. "I wouldn't exactly call Frances old."

"Kyla's not old either. And she gives me gummy worms and she tells me a joke every time I see her. Like, how do you get a Kleenex to dance?"

Ben pinched the bridge of his nose. He was losing control of the room. "How?"

"Put a little boogie in it!"

He smiled wearily. "How about inviting Joe? He loves pizza."

"I just saw Joe."

"But he does love pizza."

"Pepperoni gives him a tummy ache."

"Says who?"

"Aunt Isabel. He's not allowed to eat it."

"Okay, well, we could order something else."

"I want to invite Kyla." Gracie's eyes filled with fresh tears. It was going to be a long day for poor Tabitha.

"You're very stubborn, Gracie."

She watched him steadily.

"*Okay,*" he said, resigned. "Okay, I'll ask her, but if there's even a hint of hesitation, I'm out, got it?"

"What's hesitation?"

"When you're not sure about something."

"You don't think she'd want to come over?"

"Not because of you, because…never mind. I'll go down to the shop and ask her tonight. But if she says no, I don't want any pouting. You can ask some-one else."

"Okay, Daddy."

He waited for another second, making sure she understood, then twisted back around and put his seat belt on. How did he get himself into this again?

Looking in the rearview mirror, he felt his heart swell. She'd closed her eyes, and was leaning her head against the rest. In a minute, she'd be asleep— nothing but a sweet, snoring little girl with a tear-stained face.

She had him wrapped around her little finger. If she wanted Queen Elizabeth over for pizza, he had a feeling he'd find a way to make that happen.

He just hoped Kyla would understand. But some-thing told him he was opening a can of worms here. And not the gummy kind, either.

Kyla smiled at the barista and handed him a tip. The little coffee shop overlooking the bay was a local favorite. It opened early, and if you timed it right, you could sip your coffee while watching the fish-ing boats head out on their morning runs. On Christ-mas Eve, there was the Flotilla of Lights, where the boats were strung with lanterns, making them look like glowing pirate ships cutting through the fog. It was a tradition that dated back almost one hundred fifty years, and was how Christmas Bay had gotten its name.

This morning, though, the bay was sunny and bright, and the coffee shop wasn't overly crowded. It hummed with quiet conversation and the soft clanking of dishes. Kyla had skipped her appointment with the treadmill in order to call Marley, and since they'd be talking about Frances, she'd needed to do it away from the house.

Setting her coffee down, she sank into an overstuffed chair by the window and sighed. Her stomach was a ball of nerves. It felt like she was going behind Frances's back, which she absolutely was. But her intention was good. They needed a plan. And they needed it now.

She dug her phone out of her purse and brought up Marley's number. Her foster sister lived in Iowa, so it was later her time, and she was expecting the call. Kyla dialed and it only rang once.

"Hello?"

"Marley?"

"*Kyla!* I'm so happy to hear your voice. We shouldn't go this long without talking."

Kyla felt a familiar warmth bloom inside her chest. Stella and Marley were two of her favorite people in the world. They'd always understood her, mostly because they understood what it felt like to have lived through what she did. They got it because their stories were similar. Maybe even worse. Kyla's mother had been an addict, but at least she'd never raised a hand to Kyla. Her foster sisters couldn't say the same for their own parents.

So, they'd been brought together by Frances, and were bonded by circumstance. It was a powerful relationship, and one that Kyla treasured with her whole heart. Marley was right. They shouldn't go this long without talking again.

"I know this was kind of spur-of-the-moment," Kyla said. "I hope you weren't too busy this morning."

"No, no. I don't have to be at the ballpark until five thirty, and the game doesn't start until seven. This is a perfect time."

Marley worked for a minor league baseball team in Cedar Rapids. A baseball fan to the core, her dream was to one day be an announcer. But at the moment she was paying the bills as the assistant to the senior vice president. Mick something or other—some jerk who treated her like garbage. She couldn't stand him.

"I probably haven't said it lately," Kyla said. "But I'm so proud of you."

"Aww. I'm just trying to get my foot in the door."

"It'll happen. I know it."

"I've got my resume all polished up. I'm going to start sending it out next week before Mick the Dick decides to fire me."

"What? Why would he fire you?"

Marley made a tsking sound on the other end of the line, and Kyla could imagine her shrugging her shoulders. "Just your typical good old boy. He knows I've been trying for the announcer's job here. Jim Miller is retiring at the end of the season, so they're looking. But not looking for a woman, apparently."

"That's ridiculous."

"But par for the course. There are a lot of great people in this club, but the one in charge of hiring is a toad."

"I'm sorry, Marley."

"Don't be. I'm getting a ton of experience. I'll just keep my nose to the grindstone, and my luck's bound to change, right?"

"I know it will."

"Well," Marley said. "I'm ready. What do you need to talk to me about?"

Kyla took an even breath and looked out the window. There were a couple of kids standing on the rocks with their fishing poles in the water, a scruffy dog scratching himself at their feet. She hoped this news wasn't going to come as a total shock to her foster sister, but somehow, she didn't think it would. Stella and Marley talked to Frances all the time, and visited as often as they could. Still, it was hard to say it out loud.

She took a sip of coffee and licked the tanginess from her lips.

"Kyla?"

"Sorry. Sorry, I'm here. I just don't know how to say this. Everything's fine, Frances is fine, but since I've been back, some things have happened…"

"Like what?"

She paused, dreading this next part. "Her memory has gotten worse," she said slowly. "She got lost on a walk the other day."

Marley gasped on the other end of the line.

"She's okay," Kyla said quickly. "She got a ride, but it shook me a little. And I think it shook Frances too, but you know how she is. She'd never admit it."

"Oh, no. I've been worried about this."

"Me, too."

"I've noticed she's been forgetful lately, but I was hoping it was just stress with the shop, that kind of thing. She actually got lost? Has she been back to the doctor?"

"No, she says a diagnosis won't change anything." Kyla looked down at her coffee. "And I guess she's technically right. Except if it was Alzheimer's, there are medications she could try. Things they could do to help her prepare for the future."

"Have you talked to Stella yet?"

"No, I wanted to tell you first."

"She'd just worry anyway. Hop a plane tomorrow."

"I know, and she's between jobs, and on this road trip for the summer. I didn't want to say anything until we talked first."

Marley sighed. "Poor Frances. What are we going to do? She's up there in that huge house all alone. She can't keep *that* up."

"No. And the shop is a handful, too. I'm here for

the summer, but it's obvious she's going to need more help soon. She'll fight us on it. I don't know what to do, either."

"We'll figure it out. We made a pact, remember?"

The three of us, or none of us... She did remember. But things were different now than when they were teenagers. They all had their own lives, their own responsibilities and obligations. Plus, they were in three different states. There was nothing they wouldn't do for Frances, but sorting out the logistics wouldn't be easy.

"I know what Stella will want to do," Marley continued. "She'll want to come back. At least for a while. And if she does, that'll free you up to leave in the fall." She paused at that. "Is that what you want to do? Leave in the fall?"

Kyla chewed the inside of her cheek. "I'm not going back to Portland," she finally said. "But I wasn't planning on staying in Christmas Bay, either. I guess if Stella did come back, I could apply to some schools that are at least closer than the city was."

"Then that just leaves me."

"You've got your job."

"But I have a lot of time off coming. And maybe something will pan out so I can be closer, too. Christmas Bay has a minor league team..."

It was true, they did. But out of all three of them, Marley had always been the least interested in coming back to Oregon for good.

"Are you sure about that?" Kyla asked.

"No." Marley laughed. "But this is Frances we're talking about. We're family."

It was what Frances had always told them when they'd been nothing but their biological parents' throw-away kids. She'd say it over and over again, until their bruised and battered hearts had actually started believing it. And in time, her words had penetrated, and it was Frances who had made them come true.

They *were* family.

"We've got this," Marley continued. "The three of us, or none of us, right?"

Kyla swallowed hard. "Right."

"Consider this the Bat-Signal, Kyla Bear. By the end of the summer, one way or another, we'll be home again."

Kyla swept the floor, quietly humming to herself. She'd locked up half an hour ago, and had spent that time cleaning the bins and restocking the shelves. The sweeping didn't really have to be done tonight, but she wanted everything sparkling when Frances came in tomorrow morning. Her foster mother had always kept the shop so tidy, and Kyla wanted to alleviate as much stress for her as possible.

Leaning the broom against the wall, she turned to look out the window. The sun was sinking toward the ocean a few blocks away, turning the sky a stunning orange pink. The colors swirled around each other, reminding her of sherbet ice cream. The

YOU pick your books –
WE pay for everything.
You get up to FOUR New Books and TWO Mystery Gifts...absolutely FREE!

Dear Reader,

I am writing to announce the launch of a huge **FREE BOOKS GIVEAWAY**... and to let you know that YOU are entitled to choose up to FOUR fantastic books that WE pay for.

Try **Harlequin® Special Edition** books featuring comfort and strength in the support of loved ones and enjoying the journey no matter what life throws your way.

Try **Harlequin® Heartwarming™ Larger-Print** books featuring uplifting stories where the bonds of friendship, family and community unite.

Or **TRY BOTH!**

In return, we ask just one favor: Would you please participate in our brief Reader Survey? We'd love to hear from you.

This FREE BOOKS GIVEAWAY means that your introductory shipment is completely free, <u>even the shipping</u>! If you decide to continue, you can look forward to curated monthly shipments of brand-new books from your selected series, always at a discount off the cover price! <u>Plus you can cancel any time</u>. Who could pass up a deal like that?

Sincerely

Pam Powers

Pam Powers
For Harlequin Reader Service

Complete the survey below and return it today to receive up to 4 FREE BOOKS and FREE GIFTS guaranteed!

FREE BOOKS GIVEAWAY
Reader Survey

1
Do you prefer stories with happy endings?

◯ YES   ◯ NO

2
Do you share your favorite books with friends?

◯ YES   ◯ NO

3
Do you often choose to read instead of watching TV?

◯ YES   ◯ NO

YES! Please send me my Free Rewards, consisting of **2 Free Books from each series I select** and **Free Mystery Gifts**. I understand that I am under no obligation to buy anything, no purchase necessary see terms and conditions for details.

❏ **Harlequin® Special Edition** (235/335 HDL GRM5)
❏ **Harlequin® Heartwarming™ Larger-Print** (161/361 HDL GRM5)
❏ **Try Both** (235/335 & 161/361 HDL GRNH)

FIRST NAME   LAST NAME

ADDRESS

APT.#   CITY

STATE/PROV.   ZIP/POSTAL CODE

EMAIL ❏ Please check this box if you would like to receive newsletters and promotional emails from Harlequin Enterprises ULC and its affiliates. You can unsubscribe anytime.

SE/HW-122-FBG22_SE/HW-122-FBGVR

steady stream of tourists walking past had dwindled for the evening, as most of the shops were closed or were getting ready to close.

She'd forgotten this. How peaceful this town could be when things shut down for the night. Sometimes it felt like you were on an island all by yourself, and all the problems, all the worries of life just seemed to melt away. Christmas Bay felt safe, then. Protected.

Kyla smiled. When she was younger, it had felt less like being protected, and more like being suffocated. It was interesting how time gave you a different perspective.

Humming again, this time something softer, she picked up the broom and dustpan, and carried them into the back room. She flipped the light on, and it flooded the small space, making her blink. Unlike the shop, it was packed full of things—old boxes and wrapping paper. Mops and cleaning supplies. She really needed to talk Frances into taking a day off to help her clean it all out.

She put her hands on her hips and surveyed the Christmas decorations on the top shelf, but startled at a tapping sound coming from the front door. She looked at her watch. Past nine, and it was almost dark. Even if the sign in the window didn't say it, they were clearly closed for the night.

Turning, she walked hesitantly back into the shop. She'd shut most of the lights off when she'd locked up, but the ones that remained on made it hard to see outside. She could only make out a shadowy figure—someone wearing a black sweatshirt, and a baseball cap pulled low over his eyes. For a second, she thought it might be Hunter, but this guy was too tall. Too thick in the shoulders.

"We're closed!" she called, trying to ignore the sudden chill up her spine. "Sorry!"

The man didn't move. Just stood there watching her through the glass door.

She was temporarily frozen by the strangeness of it. Just a minute ago, she'd felt safe and secure on this sleepy little Main Street. Now its isolation felt more like an opportunity for someone with questionable motives. Or maybe she just watched too much *Dateline*.

She cleared her throat. "Sorry," she repeated. And waved for good measure. "We're closed, but we'll open at nine tomorrow!"

The man didn't move.

Behind him, a streetlamp flickered on, bathing his shoulders in a soft light. But his face, his features underneath the hat remained unrecognizable.

A truck lumbered past, its exhaust rolling into the night air, and the sputtering engine seemed to break whatever trancelike state the man was in. Slowly, he stepped away from the glass. Then turned to walk away, his gait unsteady.

Kyla watched him go with her heart in her throat. She hadn't realized she'd been holding her breath until right then. *Definitely* too much *Dateline*.

Anxious to get home now, she walked behind the

counter to grab her keys and purse. She bent down, but jumped when she heard another knock at the door and smacked her head on the counter.

"Ffffudge!"

Wincing, she straightened, expecting to see the guy in black again. Ready to pick up the phone and call the police if she had to.

But she didn't have to. Standing outside the door was Ben. His dark uniform blended into the night like her visitor's clothing from a few minutes ago, but this time its darkness felt more sexy than dangerous.

Relief flooded through her, warming her arms and legs, and making her temporarily forget the ache in her head.

He pointed at the Closed sign in the window, and mouthed *Sorry.*

"It's okay!" She grabbed her keys and unlocked the door with trembling fingers.

Frowning, he stepped past her. "Everything alright?"

"Yes. No. Yes and no. There was just a guy outside tapping on the door. Creeped me out, but he left. Then I was getting ready to leave, and when you knocked, I kind of jumped out of my skin and bumped my head on the counter." She smiled. "In a nutshell."

But he didn't smile back. Without a word, he stepped back outside and looked up and down the sidewalk. Then came back in with his jaw working.

"What did he look like?"

She shook her head, rubbing the tender spot with

her fingers. "It was too dark to see. He was wearing all black and a baseball cap. I told him we were closed, but he just stood there staring at me."

"Huh."

"Just a random weirdo, right?" The look on his face wasn't making her feel any better.

"Probably. But when you're here by yourself, especially at night, you can't be too careful. Christmas Bay isn't as safe as it used to be."

"You sound like Frances."

"How's your head?"

"It hurts."

"Here. Let me see."

He stepped closer and felt around for the lump.

"Ouch," she said miserably.

"Some Tylenol might be a good idea. Before the headache starts."

"Copy that."

He smiled down at her. "I think you're gonna make it, killer. But I'd rather you had my number, just in case."

"The dispatch number?"

He pulled out a pen and business card from his chest pocket. "My cell number," he said, writing it down. "It doesn't make sense for you to call the police and have you routed all the way through Dispatch, when I'm just a few doors down."

"When you're on duty. But what about when you're home?"

"Still not that far away. Just take it. It'll make me feel better."

She reached for the card and brushed his fingertips in the process. And there they were again—the butterflies that seemed to show up whenever Ben Martinez did.

"Thanks," she said. "I'll be responsible with it—I promise."

"Right. No prank calls in the middle of the night, or I'll know where they're coming from."

"I haven't made a prank call in at least a week. Trying to cut back."

"Sure you are."

Were they actually exchanging flirty banter? Kyla stepped behind the counter, which was a much safer place to be, considering her libido seemed to be calling all the shots here. She was supposed to be holding Ben and his sexy cop persona at an arm's length. Instead, she was apparently going to let him wrap her in his arms, and give her his personal number on the fly. Not exactly how she'd envisioned this summer panning out.

Desperate for some perspective, she reminded herself that she was perfectly capable of taking care of herself. Not only that, she *preferred* taking care of herself. And, despite how hard it was turning out to be, she was also capable of resisting whatever this was that was taking shape between them.

"What?" he asked, eyeing her.

"Nothing." She took a calming breath. "So why are you here, Ben?"

Inwardly, she winced at that. She'd overshot and sounded like an ice princess.

He didn't seem to notice. Instead, he leaned against the counter like he owned the place. This should've annoyed her, but she was too preoccupied with how his uniform shirt was stretching over his chest to care that much.

"Two things… Frances said she hired Hunter? How's that going?"

Kyla nodded. "She did. He hasn't started yet—he's going to ask his parents first. But I think it'll be okay. He seemed excited. And I talked to him about Frances, about her memory loss, so he's prepared for what that might look like. He seems like a sweet kid."

"Good. That's really good. I'll be interested to see what his parents say, though."

"You think it'll be a problem?"

"Not necessarily. But his dad's a wild card with a chip on his shoulder, so…"

Kyla frowned, thinking of what Hunter said the other day about him having a temper. "I hope this doesn't set him off."

"I'm sure it'll be fine."

"I hope so," Kyla said. "You know Frances. Once she makes up her mind…"

"I know. I'd say she's one of a kind, but I've got one at home just like her."

At the mention of Gracie, Kyla smiled. "How's she doing? Does she need a worm refill?"

"There's such a thing as a worm refill?"

"Absolutely."

"No wonder she likes you," Ben said. "Which brings me to the second reason I came by."

Kyla raised her brows.

"God." He rubbed the back of his neck. "This is going to sound weird."

"Try me."

"I told her she could have a playdate with a friend this weekend. A pizza and a movie type of thing…"

"Uh-huh…"

"And she wants to invite you."

Kyla stared at him.

"Do *not* feel like you need to come," he said quickly. "I told her that you're probably not used to being invited for playdates with six-year-olds. But like I said, she's stubborn. And I'm a pushover."

Kyla felt herself warm at that. It was one of the things that was hardest to resist about him. The way he was with his daughter.

"Anyway," he said. "I promised her I'd ask, and I asked. But now that you know, when you see her next and she mentions it, you can make something up. Say you were busy or something."

"Now, hold on. Who says I don't do playdates?"

He narrowed his eyes at her.

"It's true that I haven't had one for about twenty-five years," she said, "but that only means I'm due, right?"

"Kyla…"

"Ben."

"Are you sure?"

"I don't usually make a habit out of saying no to little girls who invite me for pizza." She shrugged. "Just saying."

"Okay… But if you change your mind, don't feel guilty about it."

"And when is this playdate?"

"Saturday. Around five. Does that work?"

"Sure. Maybe I can get Frances to close up a little early that day. Can I bring anything?"

The fact that this was sounding more and more like a date wasn't lost on her. But she pushed that thought away to concentrate on the look on his face. Nervousness, maybe a little relief. It was so endearing that her heart skipped a beat inside her chest.

"Just bring yourself," he said. "What kind of pizza do you like?"

"I'll eat anything. But I'm a sucker for pineapple."

"You and Gracie both. She'll be thrilled." His expression softened then. "Seriously. Not to get too deep into it, but she's been let down a lot lately. I really appreciate that you said yes to this. Thank you."

She smiled as he left, not trusting herself to speak. As she locked up, she realized that actually, she was kind of looking forward to it, too.

Chapter Eight

Ben pushed the squeaky shopping cart through the market with Gracie bouncing beside him. He'd had a list, but he'd forgotten it in the truck. He always forgot it in the truck.

"Ooohh! Daddy, can we get some marshmallows?"

He gritted his teeth. Every time they walked by a display of something, Gracie asked for it. She'd even asked for a can of Fancy Feast a minute ago. When he reminded her they didn't have a cat, she pointed out that Jacques counted. Kind of.

"No," he said. "We do not need any marshmallows."

"But what if Kyla wants some?"

"We're having pizza, remember?"

"But what about dessert?"

"Honey, no. And now I can't remember what I was going to get on this aisle."

"Pickles!"

"I wasn't going to get pickles."

"But we do need some."

Stifling a sigh, he leaned over and grabbed a jar of pickles. "There. I got pickles. Now let's try and get the groceries we need, not things we don't, okay?"

Gracie reached up and grabbed his hand. "Okay, Daddy."

They made their way toward the wine-and-beer section, and he eyed the stacked bottles critically. Should he get some wine? Kyla might like wine with her pizza. Then again, that might look like a date, which this wasn't. He should probably stick with soda. But he had no idea what kind of soda she liked, or whether she even liked soda, either.

"Daddy, I have to go to the bathroom."

Ben felt his shoulders slump. The grocery store potty break. He dreaded these, because there was nothing in the Divorced Dad Manual on how to handle them. And he had a tendency to do all the wrong things.

Gracie danced from foot to foot.

"Gracie, can you hold it? We're almost done, and then we'll go straight home—I promise."

She crossed her legs. "Okay."

"If you really have to go, we can park the cart, and I'll take you."

"No, I can hold it."

He watched her for a few seconds to make sure.

"I can hold it, Daddy," she said again. "But when we get back to the car, you'll have to floor it."

"Copy that."

They made their way down the next aisle, and the next, and then finally, arrived at the checkout line.

Gracie seemed to have forgotten that she had to go to the bathroom, and was now staring up at a *National Enquirer* with a teenage popstar on the cover.

"What does *baby mama* mean, Daddy?"

A woman in line snickered, and Ben's neck heated. "Nothing."

Gracie had been reading since kindergarten. An idea of Isabel's he once thought brilliant, until he realized that his daughter could now read all the tabloid headlines in the checkout line. And he'd have to explain them.

"It says, 'Tucker's baby mama pregnant with twins,'" she said. Loudly. "What does *pregnant* mean?"

More snickers from behind them. Ben inched the cart forward, praying the checker would pick up the pace, which at the moment, felt absolutely glacial.

"It means getting ready to have a baby," he said, his voice low.

"How do you get to have a baby?"

He looked down at her. Really? *Really?* He was facing the birds-and-bees question in a grocery store checkout line, with no less than ten people listening in? His luck really couldn't get any worse. No, wait.

That wasn't true. Gracie could always remember she had to go to the bathroom and not make it to the car.

He bent down and whispered in her ear. "I'll tell you when we get home, okay?" Or, when she turned fifteen. Either, or.

"Okay."

Two people started arguing in the next line over. Ben straightened to see, forgetting about Gracie's question for a second, and focusing on the sound of their voices. Raised. Agitated.

"I saw you put it in your pocket," the checker said to a man whose back was turned. But the slant of his shoulders looked familiar.

Ben stiffened.

"I didn't take shit," the man said.

"If you don't empty your pockets, I'm calling Security."

The other people in line backed up, obviously uncomfortable.

Ben scooted Gracie behind him, ready to park her in a safe spot in case he needed to step in.

"Oh, you mean *this*?" the man said, pulling a phone case from his pocket. "I was going to pay for it. I forgot."

Eying him warily, the checker snatched the case back. "Don't come back or we'll charge you with trespassing."

Gracie tugged on his hand. "What's happening, Daddy? Why are they mad?"

"Shhh, honey. I need to keep an eye on the situation, okay?"

The man held his hands in the air in mock surrender. "I'm going. I'm going. Keep your panties on."

He turned then and Ben could see him clearly.
And his voice, the familiar slant to his shoulders,
all clicked into place. *Gabe Mohatt.*

Ben watched him with his jaw working. With his
gut tight. The guy was trouble, but more than that, he
was unpredictable. Ben had felt it from the first time
he'd had to arrest him, drunk and disorderly a year
ago. He had the distinct feeling that the issues with
Hunter's dad were escalating; he just couldn't put his
finger on what they were escalating *to* yet. It concerned him, for Hunter's sake. For his mother's sake,
who Ben knew had tried to leave before, thanks to
the police reports. And now for Frances's and Kyla's
sakes, too.

Was it enough to keep Hunter from working at
Coastal Sweets? No, because there wasn't any proof
of anything yet. And besides, having an abusive dad
wasn't Hunter's fault. But it did mean that Ben would
be watching the shop even closer from now on. Assuming Hunter even lasted there.

Gabe Mohatt turned on the people watching him.
And then his gaze landed on Ben, a look of slow recognition settling over his face. He grinned.

And it was chilling.

Kyla pulled up to the curb in front of the green
ranch house, and leaned across the seat to check the
address—1616. Talent Avenue. This was it. And if
there'd been any doubt, there was a pink bike in the

driveway, and some little rain boots sitting by the front door.

Taking a steadying breath, she unbuckled her seat belt. Ben had told her not to bring anything, but years of Frances's etiquette lessons had taken their toll. She reached for the fat bag of gummy worms she'd brought from the shop, and tucked them in her purse. They were technically for Gracie, but they worked for Ben, too. Who wouldn't want gummy worm appetizers? Well…a lot of people. So, she had some chocolates too, just in case.

She stepped out of the car and glanced around. It was a nice, mature neighborhood, full of houses that had been built in the fifties or sixties. It was several blocks from the ocean, but was a typical Oregon coast beach house, with a big twisting cedar in the yard, surrounded by hardy tufts of beach grass.

The breeze blew Kyla's hair across her face, and she reached up to tuck it behind her ear. She was nervous. And kept trying to talk herself out of being nervous, because this was just a playdate. Which was ridiculous, because it wasn't really a playdate because she was thirty years old, but still. Despite lecturing herself on the drive over, her stomach still felt like she was on a veritable roller-coaster ride— dipping and falling with every thought of Ben.

She tucked her purse underneath her arm, and headed up the walkway toward the front door. But before she could raise her hand to knock, it swung open wide. Gracie stood there wearing a tutu and a gap-toothed grin.

"Hi!"

Kyla grinned back. It was impossible not to. "Hi there. I brought you something. Close your eyes."

Gracie squeezed them shut and reached both hands out as if she was used to this game.

"Here. Don't eat them all at once—got it?"

Gracie jumped up and down. *"Worms!"*

Kids were so easy to please.

"Come on," Gracie said, grabbing her hand. "I want to show you my room."

"Let her catch her breath, kiddo." Ben appeared behind his daughter, looking gorgeous in a pair of jeans and an Oregon State T-shirt. Really, he'd look gorgeous in anything, but the T-shirt was especially understated and sexy, accenting his broad shoulders, and offering just a hint of his muscled biceps underneath the sleeves.

Kyla looked away, hoping he hadn't noticed her staring. Instead, she made a point of glancing around the house, immediately loving its midcentury modern style. Sometimes houses like this could feel cold, but this one was cozy. Lots of color and softness, with a big cushy sectional in the living room that drew your eyes toward the built-in bookcases on either side of the TV. It was a comfortable space that begged to be lived in, and Kyla felt some of her nerves easing away a little.

"This is a great house, Ben."

"Thanks. It was actually my uncle Miguel's. He sold it to us when he moved to Bellingham. It needed some updating, but the bones were great."

Kyla nodded, assuming the *us* in that statement meant him and his ex-wife. Again, she wondered who could walk away from a life like this—a lovely house, a beautiful family. There was a time when she would've given her right arm for such a happy ending. Of course, the reality was she had no idea what kind of marriage they'd had. Maybe Ben snored, or left the toilet seat up. Maybe he had some secret addiction that turned him into a different person when the sun went down. But she doubted it. He was probably just as perfect as she'd always thought he was.

Gracie tugged on her hand again. "I can show you my Barbies!"

"You're going to rip her arm out of the socket, Gracie," Ben said. "Slow down."

Kyla laughed, letting herself be pulled down the hallway. "It's okay," she said over her shoulder. "Makes me feel like a big deal."

Gracie's room was adorable. Her princess bed was basically a giant version of Jacques's, only with a pink canopy and no cat hair.

The little girl immediately launched herself onto the mattress and began jumping up and down. The excitement was strong with this one.

"Gracie," Ben said from the doorway. "No jumping on the bed."

She climbed obligingly down, and sat cross-legged on the carpet. Then patted the spot next to her.

Kyla sat down too, crossing her legs like Gracie. She felt like she was in elementary school again, getting ready to listen to a story after lunch.

"Okay," Ben said. "I'm going to order the pizza. Delivery always takes longer on the weekends."

Kyla's stomach rumbled. All of a sudden, pizza sounded delicious. "We'll just be here having a Barbie meeting," she said. "Important business."

"Yeah," Gracie chimed in. "Super important!"

Ben winked at her. Then looked over at Kyla with a sparkle in his eyes that almost made her forget that once upon a time, he'd been her biggest heartbreak.

Almost.

Ben walked over to where Gracie was asleep on the couch, and scooped her warm little body up in his arms.

"Be right back," he whispered to Kyla, who was sipping a cup of coffee a few feet away.

It had been a nice evening, but an exhausting one for Gracie, who'd crashed after pizza and half of *Frozen*.

Ben carried her to her room now, and deposited her on her bed, where she immediately curled into a ball. He didn't have the heart to wake her to brush her teeth. She'd just have to make up for it in the morning.

Covering her with her fuzziest blanket, he reached for Henry the Hippo and tucked him in next to her.

Then bent to give her a kiss on the temple. She smelled like baby powder, her lashes dark smudges against her cheeks.

"Good night, kiddo," he said softly.

He walked out, and pulled her door halfway closed behind him. She liked the light, and he liked knowing he'd be able to hear her if she woke in the middle of the night.

Kyla looked up as he came back into the living room, his feet padding on the hardwood floor.

"Is she all tucked in?"

"All tucked in and all wiped out," he said. "I don't think I've seen her this excited…maybe ever. You made her entire year."

"That's hard to believe. I'm probably a hugely boring playdate. I could barely stand up after Barbies."

He laughed, and sat down next to her. "Tell me about it. That's trying to keep up with a six-year-old in a nutshell."

"She's so cute. You've done a wonderful job with her."

She looked away then. Ben watched her, noticing how with the fading light outside, her eyes seemed darker. Her hair hung next to her face, practically begging for him to push it away. His hands itched with it.

Instead, he leaned back on the couch and rubbed them down his thighs. "How's your head?"

"My head?"

"The bump from the other night?"

"Oh," she said. "Better. There's still a little knot there, but it's not bad. I let Gracie feel it. She was intrigued."

"She likes injuries, just as long as they're not her own."

"Well. Naturally."

Kyla had been amazing with Gracie this afternoon. She obviously had a way with kids, which made sense, since she was a teacher.

Ben had found himself listening to them from the other room, feeling a mixture of gratitude toward Kyla, and anger at Sam. Gracie was clearly hungry for a mother figure in her life. She'd said she wanted a playdate, but what she really wanted was someone who would look at her Barbies and her dresses, who would listen to her make up stories about her dolls. Someone who might fill a void that as hard as Ben might try, he'd never be able to. It made him sad. And it made him feel protective of his daughter, who would definitely get attached if he let her.

Working his jaw, he glanced over at Kyla again, suddenly annoyed with himself for letting things get this far. Of course Gracie was going to get attached. Then what? She wouldn't understand the difference between a playmate and whatever Kyla might become in her heart. She'd only feel hurt and confusion when she left at the end of the summer.

Isabel would tell him he was being ridiculous, that this was only one afternoon. But if how he felt about her was any indication, Gracie would be falling just as hard. And Kyla was still a complete mystery to them both. Someone whose intentions weren't clear, and whose time in Christmas Bay was ticking.

It all meant that he had no business wanting to push her hair away from her face. He had no business wanting to touch her at all. What he needed to do was fulfill his promise to Frances—he'd look in on her like he'd said he would, but after that, it was time to put some distance between himself and Kyla Beckett.

She looked at him, her pretty mouth turned down at the sides. "Are you okay? You seem quiet."

"Fine. Just thinking."

"About?"

"Gracie mostly." He swallowed hard, trying to decide how much to say. The problem with Kyla was that he wanted to tell her more than he probably should. She had that way about her.

She leaned forward and put her mug down on the coffee table. Then turned to face him, tucking her hands in her lap. "Do you feel like talking about it? I know you're probably ready to kick me out, but I still have a little more coffee left, and it'd be a shame to waste it."

She smiled, and for the second time since sitting down next to her, he had the urge to reach for her. What was he supposed to say? *I really want to kiss you, Kyla, but I know you still resent me, and I don't want you disappointing my daughter when you leave, because you're absolutely the leaving kind.*

Maybe that last part wasn't fair, but he was beyond rationalizing at this point. Still, she continued watching him with those storm cloud eyes, the ones that always seemed to be able to see right inside him. Even when she'd been a little girl.

Before he realized what he was doing, he did reach for her. He took her hand, and gently squeezed her fingers.

He could tell he'd surprised her. Which was fine, because he'd shocked the hell out of himself.

"I'm going to be honest with you," he said quietly. "Because after everything that's happened, that's the least I can do."

Her hand was soft in his, giving. She didn't stiffen or try to pull away. She just sat there, letting him open himself up to her, even if it was just the smallest amount.

"We used to know each other pretty well, and I've always cared about you," he continued. "And for some weird reason, I always felt responsible for you. I guess because of what I did—and to be honest, I still do. I know that sounds crazy, believe me. But it's how I feel."

She nodded.

"But sometime over the last few weeks, that feeling has turned into something else, and I'm not quite sure what to do about it, except the thing that makes the most sense, which is pull away a little. For some perspective. And I think that'd be a horrible thing to do without telling you why first."

"Ben…"

"Just let me say this. Before I change my mind."

Again, she nodded.

He licked his lips and rubbed his thumb over her knuckles. "Watching you with Gracie tonight… It was hard. It's just been the two of us for a while now, and that's okay. At least, that's what I've been telling myself, until I saw the look on her face when you pulled up to the house. And my heart. It broke my damn heart."

Kyla frowned, leaning closer. He was making her feel bad for him, which wasn't what he wanted. He didn't want her sympathy. He wanted her to understand where he was coming from.

Frustrated, he cleared his throat. "The bottom line is, I have to protect her. She has to come first."

"Because you're a good man," she said.

Was that what he was? He wasn't sure. At the end of the day, he'd simply tried to lead with his heart and do the best by people that he could. Kyla had taught him that lesson early on. When he'd barely been old enough to learn it.

But now, here he was, denying what his heart wanted most. Which was to get to know her. Spend some time with her. Kiss her. And that felt less like being honest, and more like being afraid.

Slowly, he pulled his hand away. It didn't matter anyway. He meant what he said. Gracie had to come first, and that meant he didn't have the luxury of getting to know Kyla, or anyone else for that matter. So. This was the perspective he'd needed. Arriving just in time.

"You don't trust me," she said, her voice low.

"I'm sorry?"

She watched him steadily. "You don't trust that I feel the same way. And if I do, that I won't eventually cause you pain."

What could he say to that? Since it was 100 percent true. So, he didn't say anything at all.

"I know the words to this song, Ben," she continued. "I've been singing it my whole life. Who am I if I'm not the person afraid to trust someone again? Because trusting people never ends well. That's what you and I have learned, right?"

He gritted his teeth, feeling the muscles in his jaw flex almost painfully. "That's true," he said.

She put her hand on his thigh. Its weight felt good there, natural. Like he'd been waiting for its warmth this whole time.

"So," she said. "We're a match made in hell."

"Basically."

"And we're going to stay away from each other from now on."

"Probably wise."

"And are we still being honest?"

He nodded.

"You're making it really hard not to fall in love with you again," she said.

The room was dim, but he could see her lovely face well enough. Could see that her cheeks had flushed at that, and despite how bold the statement just was, she lowered her lashes.

He waited a beat. Maybe two, because he was still trying to process the words…*in love with you again*.

After a minute, she looked up. "I can't even blame wine for this," she said quietly. "Coffee was too sensible, Ben."

He'd always been sensible. It was a blessing and a curse. This conversation was sensible. Pulling his hand away from hers was sensible. The way he wanted to ease her back on the couch, and kiss that hollow spot at the base of her throat, was definitely *not* sensible.

So what was he going to do about it?

Chapter Nine

Kyla wasn't altogether sure she wasn't going to pass out. She could almost feel the blood rushing through her veins—it roared in her ears, making her dizzy.

Or maybe that was Ben making her dizzy. At the moment, it was impossible to tell. She'd only kept one true secret her entire life, and that was from the man sitting beside her now. Only, right then, she could only see him as a teenager—in his letterman's jacket, wearing that dazzling smile. *Ben*. Her only love. And how could that be after all these years? After leaving Christmas Bay full of brand-new strength and a rock-solid sense of self?

Maybe she wasn't as strong as she thought she was, if those carefully constructed walls crumbled in one night.

She forced a breath, pulling the air into her lungs and letting it slowly out again. *Her Ben.* But that was an ironic thought, because he'd never been hers at all.

"What did you say?" he asked.

And now, naturally, she'd be expected to answer. It wasn't too late to try and gather her wits and lighten the mood—to make some kind of joke out of it. After all, this was ancient history, right?

But the thing was, it wasn't. It had affected her for too long, and in too many ways. It was still affecting her. *He* was still affecting her. And for some reason that she couldn't quite understand, she needed to talk about this. It felt good to finally release it, and release it to him.

She sat up straighter. And this time, spoke with conviction. "I loved you, Ben."

"You loved me…" he repeated.

"I was only a kid. But it was more than just a crush. I can't deny that anymore."

"I had no idea."

"You wouldn't have. You were so much older than me. You didn't even know I was alive."

"I knew you were alive."

"Because you always watched out for me. I never had that at home. I thought you were the bravest boy I knew. You were my hero."

He frowned then. "Until you were taken away."

When she felt her hands begin to shake, she clasped them together in her lap, squeezing hard to ground herself. "I didn't know how to reconcile those things.

All those wonderful things about you, with feeling like you threw me away."

"Threw you away? Kyla…"

"That's how I felt. My home life wasn't great, but at least I knew what to expect. My mom was an addict and there weren't very many surprises there, either. But being taken away from her was terrifying. I didn't know where they were going to put me. I didn't know if it would be worse. And I missed her…"

Without warning, she felt the sting of tears. Talking about her mom always did this to her. Always.

"And then she died," she continued. "Before I got to go back. Before she could heal herself enough to get me back. I never knew if she *would've* been able to heal herself for me. And I was so mad at you, it scared me. I loved you, but then I hated you. And I hated myself, too. For not running away and going back to her."

"Kyla," he said again. This time softer. And this time he was the one who reached for her. He cupped her cheek in his hand, rubbing the pad of his thumb over her cheekbone. His touch was so gentle that it made her light-headed.

"Look at me," he said.

She did. But even now, even as she felt herself leaning into his touch, she wanted to lean away. Ben was a complication she didn't need. She'd spent a lot of time trying to get right after leaving Christmas Bay. She couldn't go back to being so terribly unsure of things. She just couldn't.

"If hating me is what you need to get through this," Ben said, his voice low, "then hate me. I can take it. Just as long as you don't hate yourself."

She stared up at him. Nobody had ever had the effect on her that he did. Nobody. It was one of those absolutes in her life, like the sky being blue or the sun coming up in the east. He would always have some kind of pull over her, some kind of sway. She knew that, just like she knew she'd probably stop fighting this eventually. Even if it was for a moment or two. A temporary clearing in a stormy sky.

He tucked her hair behind her ear, and his gaze dropped to her mouth. She could almost feel it resting there as if it were a tangible thing.

"This is a bad idea," he whispered. "Neither one of us is in the right place for it."

He was protecting her, even now. She loved it. And she didn't want to love it.

Suddenly grasping on to all the grown-up strength and independence she'd managed to nurture these last few years, she reached up and took his face in her hands. She didn't need him to tell her what was right for her. Even if he was the worst idea that ever was, *she* wanted to be the one to make that call.

So, she leaned forward and placed her lips on his. Tasting him, drawing in his warmth and scent. Letting her heart gallop away inside her chest. And not letting herself think about it, or care about the consequences. She had plenty of time for that later. Now she just wanted to be kissed back.

With a low sound inside his throat, he reached around her waist and pulled her close. After all his talking, there wasn't an ounce of hesitation in his movement. Only desire. Only need.

Kyla knew she could get used to this, to be held like this. To be wanted like this. It only made her want to stoke the fire more, to see how hot it would burn.

She pressed herself even closer. He was long and lean, with sinewy muscle in his thighs, shoulders and arms. She laid her hand against his chest and splayed her fingers out, feeling one of his hardened nipples through his T-shirt.

He let out a ragged breath, kissing her, moving his hand up the back of her sweater. When she felt its heat on her skin, she arched her back instinctively.

He kissed along her jawline, and then down the side of her neck, exploring her with a skill that sent chills up her arms.

She shivered, unable to help it, and he pulled away with a frown. "Are you cold?"

"No. In fact, I was wishing I hadn't worn this dumb sweater."

"It's gonna rain later. You might be glad you did."

"I doubt it."

Slowly, he rearranged her sweater over her jeans. Then ran his hand lightly over the curve of her bottom before easing himself away a few inches.

Her heart squeezed. *Okay*, she thought. *He's right. Stop before we do something we regret.* Still, she couldn't help but wonder what he was thinking right then. His expression had shuttered, his eyes darkening in a way that made it impossible to tell.

"Gracie has a habit of waking up and asking for water after I put her to bed," he said. "I wouldn't be surprised if she wandered in here looking for us..."

Kyla leaned back too, fighting the ache in her throat. It was harder than she'd ever imagined, having to pull away from him. But to give him credit, he'd tried to put the brakes on. She'd been the one to plow right through.

Maybe it was Gracie he was worried about, and maybe it wasn't. It didn't really matter, though, because this was obviously for the best. She ran a hand over her hair, hoping she didn't look how she felt—like a woman lusting over a man who had no intention of trusting her with his heart.

"I used to do that, too," she said with a small smile. "Call for water in the middle of the night. Only my mom usually slept right through it. I just got used to being thirsty."

He wore that unreadable expression again. And she was afraid if she sat there too long, he might touch her again, and she didn't think she'd be able to stop herself with just a kiss this time. No, best just to walk away with her dignity intact. With her head on semistraight, and chalk this up to a fantasy that had been a reality for a few short minutes, and that was that.

"I'd better get going," she said. "It's getting late, and Hunter's going to be at the shop first thing in the morning. I have a feeling I'll need all the sleep I can get."

She stood up, and he did, too, his height making her feel small next to him.

Putting his hands in his jean pockets, he waited while she picked up her purse and put it over her shoulder. The muscles in his jaw bunched and relaxed, and he reminded her of a caged tiger right then. All power and pent-up energy. She wondered if when she left, he might start pacing the floor.

"You have my number?" he asked. "In case you need me tomorrow?"

She nodded. "I've got it."

"And you'll use it?"

"I promise."

She headed to the front door, trying to ignore how heavy her feet felt. How her heart felt heavier. She'd use his number if she needed him. But she was going to try her best not to need him at all.

She reached for the doorknob, but he put a hand on her shoulder, stopping her.

"Kyla…"

Turning, she looked up at him again. He was gorgeous in the dim light of the room, his dark hair curling just a little over his ears. His scruffy jaw making her think of how it had felt scraping against her skin just a few minutes ago.

"Yes?"

"This?" he said. "Tonight? It was all on me. If it was a mistake, it was my mistake."

This was so like him. Even wanting to take the discomfort of regret away from her.

"No, Ben. You don't get to do that. I kissed you, remember?"

His expression softened some. His eyes took her in with that characteristic warmth she remembered so well. But there was a distinct distance now. A distance that he'd created. Or maybe she was the one who needed that distance to get out the door.

"You're a strong woman, Kyla," he said.

Her stomach dropped. It was what she'd always wanted to be. As much as she'd loved her mother, as much as she'd missed her when she'd gone, she'd also been a tangle of weakness and fear and uncertainty. And those things had doomed their time together.

To hear this from Ben, someone she still thought was the bravest boy she knew, it took the breath from her lungs. Instead of answering, she stood on her tiptoes and kissed him on the cheek.

And then walked out the door, before she could do anything else.

The next morning dawned foggy and cold. There was light rain in the forecast for later. Ben had been right about the sweater.

Kyla stood in front of the cash register, pushing the image of Ben away for what must have been the tenth time that hour. It was Hunter's very first day, and he was excited and nervous, and he deserved all of her attention.

He turned to her now, wearing a shy smile. "Like this?"

She was teaching him how to ring someone up. They'd decided to lock the doors and hang a sign up that said Training, so the shop was peaceful and empty. He'd come in wearing a button-down shirt, and jeans without holes in them. Kyla's heart had squeezed when she'd seen him, and she had to wonder if he'd bought these clothes especially for his first day of work.

He'd handed over his application, and told her that his mom had given him her blessing. When Kyla had asked about his dad, he'd only said he was glad for another paycheck in the house.

As much as that prickled at her, she figured it was good enough. As long as he wasn't mad at Hunter for being here, she could live with knowing he wasn't necessarily proud of his son for showing up. *She* was proud of him. And she intended to tell him every day.

She smiled back. "Just like that," she said. "You're doing great."

"I'm nervous."

She could tell. Whenever he picked up the money to practice making change, she could see his hands shake. It got her right in the feelers, as Gracie would say.

"That's totally normal. And we won't be putting you behind the counter for a while yet, anyway. I'm just showing you the ropes so you know what to expect when we do. And when that time comes, either Frances or I will be here in case you need help."

He pushed his mop of hair away from his forehead. "Where is she this morning?"

Since Kyla had told him about Frances's dementia, Hunter had taken a special interest in her. He had a lot of questions, and seemed concerned about her well-being. It was very sweet, and Kyla had to wonder if he'd ever had anyone close to him suffer memory loss. He hadn't mentioned it, but she knew from experience that kids weren't going to necessarily volunteer information that was painful for them. She just knew that in time, if this job worked out and he stayed on for a while, she'd learn more about him when he was ready.

"She's taking the morning off," Kyla said. "She'll be in around noon with Jacques."

Hunter grinned at mention of the cat. When she'd told him earlier that Jacques was usually camped out on the counter, he'd confessed that he'd never had a pet before. But he *had* been able to take care of the class hamster over vacation once, and that was pretty cool. Judging by the look on his face, Jacques might end up being one of his favorite things about working at Coastal Sweets.

"So," she said, "do you feel like you know how to count change back?"

"I think so."

She nodded, reaching in front of him to close the

cash register. "And by the way, you look nice today. Very sharp."

He tugged on his collar. "It's a little scratchy. But my mom said it would make a good impression."

"Your mom's a smart lady. But if you're more comfortable in a T-shirt or something, that's great, too. Frances isn't picky. When I was your age, I used to come to work in sweatshirts and jeans."

He turned to her, his blue eyes wide. "You used to work here?"

"Frances is my foster mom. I worked here in high school. But then I moved away for college."

"Oh. So, do you like, work here for good now?"

"Just for the summer to help out. I'm a teacher."

"That's cool. What do you teach?"

"History," she said. "Do you like history?"

"I like math the best. History is kind of boring. I mean, I'm sure *you're* not boring…"

She smiled.

"Some of it's okay," he continued. "I like to learn about wars and stuff."

"Well, there you go. A history buff in the making."

He smiled back, looking skeptical, but like he didn't want to hurt her feelings.

"Here," she said. "Why don't I show you where all the cleaning products are. You'll have to clean the windows and the bins two or three times a day. Lots of sticky little fingers all over everything."

He followed her to the back room and watched as she pointed out the bucket with the Windex and rags.

"We keep most everything back here," she said. "But if you can't find anything, just ask. Sometimes Frances moves things and forgets where she puts them."

He nodded, looking around. After a minute, they headed back into the shop where she plucked her front door keys off the counter and jingled them.

"Ready?" she asked. "You'll pick it up fast—I can tell."

"I hope so. I don't want to look like a jerk on my first day."

"You're not going to look like a jerk."

He tugged at his collar again. Then frowned, an expression settling over his face that made her pause.

She put her keys back down on the counter. "What is it?"

"I was just thinking about what you said before."

"About?"

"About you being a foster kid…"

She watched him. There was a tone to his voice that hadn't been there before. The slightest trembling in his vocal cords.

"I was," she said. "Frances finished raising me."

He was quiet for a minute, picking at a hangnail on his thumb.

"Why were you wondering about that?" she asked.

He shrugged. "I got taken away from my parents a long time ago, but they got me back. It's no big deal—I hardly remember it. I was really little."

But she could tell he did. And she felt so strongly

for him right then, it was hard not to give him a hug. She knew all about the deflection, the denial, the shrugging of the shoulders and acting like it didn't matter. But it did. It mattered. All of it mattered.

She swallowed hard, not wanting to say anything that would embarrass him for telling her. She knew about the embarrassment, too. But there was a reason he'd said something. Maybe he needed a connection to someone who understood.

"It was hard," she finally said. "It was very hard on me. But I had friends who had it harder. I got lucky with Frances. But I never got to go home again."

He continued picking at his thumb, and she worried it might start to bleed. All the cuticles around his fingernails were ragged and torn. So, he'd been a foster kid, too. She had to wonder if he was anything like she'd been as a girl, praying for something to change. For anything to change.

Her prayers had eventually been answered, but not in the way she'd hoped for. She'd been granted a guardian angel in Ben Martinez, and he'd proceeded to turn her world inside out.

"I liked my foster parents," Hunter said. "They were nice to me."

She frowned. "What about your parents? Are they nice to you?"

It was a bold question, but at this point, she didn't care. He'd already spoken volumes, even though he might not know it yet.

"My mom is great. It's not her fault. She's tried to…"

"She's tried to what?"

Hunter's eyes grew distant, and she knew he was done talking about it. "Nothing," he said. "Nothing."

And there was the wall. She knew about those, too.

Chapter Ten

Ben sat next to Isabel at the only table at Mario's overlooking the ocean. It was the restaurant's most coveted spot, and when they'd walked in, Isabel had practically squealed at their luck.

She gazed out at the sunset now—a brilliant pink-and-purple number tonight. The clouds from earlier had thinned and cleared, and were now only wispy sponges of heavenly color.

Looking over at him, she smiled. "Did you order?"

"Large pepperoni. Man, we eat a lot of pizza."

She laughed. "That's what happens when you have kids. All pizza, all the time."

"I love pizza. But you know. Maybe not for *every* meal."

"Dream on, big brother. It'll be like this until Gracie leaves for college."

At the thought of his baby growing up enough to leave for anywhere, his chest tightened. He glanced over at her now. She was playing one of the arcade games with her cousins—something with lots of blinking lights and obnoxious beeping sounds.

He picked up his beer and took a long sip. Then set it down again and licked some foam from his lips.

"Speaking of pizza," Isabel said evenly. "I can't believe you didn't tell me about this playdate the other day."

Ben froze, caught off guard. Although, why the hell he was surprised like that, he didn't know. Even if Gracie hadn't said anything, one of his neighbors probably would've. He lived across the street from a nosey retiree named Larry, who made a habit out of asking him about his love life to an almost offensive degree.

After a second, he sighed and sat back in his chair. "She told you."

"Well, of course she told me. She's six. She told everyone."

"Everyone?"

"Ben. She's six."

"I know, I know. Still…"

Isabel shifted so she was facing him. She crossed her legs, and leaned her elbows on the table, looking like she was settling in for the long haul. Perfect.

"So, are you going to tell me," she said, "or am I going to have to get the skinny at the supermarket?"

"You're overestimating how much people care."

"Ha. That's rich. You know people care. Even if they didn't care, *I* care, and I should've been the first to know. But I digress…"

"I didn't tell you, because there's nothing to tell. Gracie wanted to have a playdate, and after I told her she could invite whoever she wanted, she said she wanted to invite Kyla."

Isabel grinned. "Go on."

"It's not funny."

"I didn't say it was. Go on."

"So, I tried to talk her out of it, but you know Gracie."

"Stubborn as a mule?"

"Basically. And I didn't have the heart to say no, so I told her I'd ask Kyla, figuring she'd come up with some kind of excuse."

"But she didn't."

"No. She didn't."

Isabel leaned back, acting like she wasn't surprised by any of this. "So, how was it?"

"It was, you know…" He looked down at his beer, rubbing some of the condensation off with his thumb. "It was fine. It was good."

Isabel stared at him.

"It was good," he said again, feeling his neck heat. He looked back up at her. "I don't know what else you want me to say."

"Good grief, Ben. I know there's more to it than that."

"How do you know there's more?"

"Because I saw the two of you at Joe's party, remember? I can tell you like her."

"Everyone likes her. She's a nice person."

Isabel leaned forward, her eyes bright. "Exactly. This is okay, you know. Having her over. Getting to know her. Liking her…"

He glanced over at the kids, making sure they were still out of earshot.

When he turned back to his sister, he took an even breath. "I'm not sure how you can really say that, Isabel. Knowing how things turned out with Sam."

"But she's not Sam."

"No, but Gracie loves her. I couldn't get her to stop talking about her all week. That's a problem."

"You're not going to *marry* her."

"Exactly. But Gracie doesn't understand that. I can't let her get attached to someone who isn't going to stick around."

Isabel pursed her lips, looking frustrated. He didn't care. He was frustrated, too.

"First of all," she said, "you don't know she's not sticking around. Second, don't you see how screwed up that kind of thinking is?"

He watched her, gritting his teeth.

"You don't want her to get attached to Kyla," she continued, "because you don't want her to get hurt. But *not* letting her form attachments to people is hurting her too, Ben."

He looked out at the ocean and took another long swallow of his beer. It was hard to argue with that kind of logic. Mostly because it was true. He understood that it didn't make any sense, but it didn't have to. He only wanted what was best for his daughter.

"I'm sorry," Isabel finally said. "I know I'm pushing. It's just hard to see you so closed off. You're not a distant person. This isn't like you."

"People change. They learn from their mistakes. They finally get a damn clue."

"They get damaged."

He shot her a look.

"You can have a future with someone again," she continued quietly. "You can be happy."

"With Kyla?" He laughed, and he didn't like how bitter it sounded. "She trusts people less than I do."

"I'm not saying with Kyla. But if you gave somebody a chance, maybe they'd surprise you. Maybe she'd surprise you."

They watched each other through the dim light of the pizza parlor, letting that settle between them. The kids were giggling now, and the warm smell of bread and cheese wafted through the restaurant. Ben's stomach growled, reminding him that he hadn't eaten all day. He hadn't even been hungry until right then. Too busy thinking. Too busy painting himself right into a corner.

"Just think about what I'm saying," Isabel said. "For me."

There was actually nothing he wanted less, than to think about it and realize maybe she was right.

Isabel was right about a lot of things. But this…this hit too close to home for comfort.

He sighed, running his hand through his hair, which was getting a little too long. Sam used to cut his hair for him, and ever since then, he hated getting it done. Too many memories.

"I guess," he said evenly. "I guess I'll think about it."

She gave him a hopeful smile. "That's all I'm asking. Keep the door open. Just a crack, okay?"

Before he could answer, the kids came running. Gracie threw her arms around his neck and gave him a sloppy kiss on the cheek.

"What were you guys talking about?"

"Nothing," he said.

"Can we get ice cream after?"

There was a cute little ice-cream parlor right down the street from the station. It was Gracie's favorite place for sugar, aside from Coastal Sweets.

He looked at his watch. If they didn't take forever with the pizza, they could probably make it for an ice-cream cone before closing.

"If you eat all your dinner, I'll think about it."

She clasped her hands together. "Can Joe and Lucas come?"

"Aww, we can't, honey," Isabel said. "We promised their grandma Ruth we'd stop by later. I think she's planning on giving them dessert."

"Shoot. It's just me and you, Daddy."

She squeezed his neck again, and he patted her warm little hand.

It was just them. Maybe it always would be.

Gracie ran up ahead, skipping over the cracks in the sidewalk. Ben kept an eye on her, making sure she didn't go too far like she had a tendency to do. Or that she didn't run into some unsuspecting tourist with their arms full of bags.

He put his hands in his pockets, feeling the chill of the evening move over his bare arms. The waves crashed in the distance. The tide would be going out now, pulled by the force of the moon, and leaving just a glimpse of the ocean floor glistening underneath its silver light.

Gracie stopped, peering into a shop window with her nose pressed against the glass. Her hair had gotten a little longer over the last month, her bangs evening out, thank God. But she still looked so small standing there, that his heart caught in his throat.

She turned, making sure he was still coming. He waved, and she waved back, impatient. What would he ever do without Gracie? What would she do without him? The thought kept him up at night. Christmas Bay was a small town, but he still had a dangerous job. The truth was, anything could happen at any time. That was life. And like Isabel said, was it fair to keep her from other kinds of love, even if there was risk that went along with it?

He knew the answer to that—it wasn't.

"Evening, Chief."

He glanced over to see a city councilman walking by with his wife. Leo and Alice Van Meter. They also owned a tire shop out on the highway. Nice people.

He smiled. "Hey there."

"Pretty night," Leo said.

"It is."

"There's a storm coming, though," Alice said. "Lots of wind. Not great for my hair."

Ben laughed. "I'm sure it'll hold up."

Storms were rare this late in the season—usually by March their strongest ones had subsided. Hopefully the wind wouldn't be as bad as it could get during the winter months, but they'd be prepared anyway.

He nodded at them as they passed, feeling an unexpected contentment settle over him for the first time in a while. Weather aside, he could never understand why Sam wanted to leave here so badly. Even if she hadn't had a family who loved her. Sure, it was a small community, and all small communities had their fair share of problems. But this was such a nice place to live. Such a nice place to raise kids. Of course, raising kids hadn't turned out to be a priority of hers, so what the hell did he know?

He slowed, realizing they were already at the ice-cream parlor, and looked up to call Gracie back, but she was nowhere in sight. His stomach dropped. She knew not to wander out of his sight; he'd told her a million times. But she was also a kid, and he hadn't been watching her just now, which was on him.

That warm feeling disappeared just as fast as it had come. He craned his neck trying to see past a small group of people coming out of a restaurant a few yards away.

With his heart in his throat, he pushed past the crowd as politely as he could manage. The downside to being a police officer was knowing exactly how many bad people were out there, just waiting for an opportunity. Yes, there were a lot of good ones, too. In fact, he believed the majority of them were good, like the Van Meters just now. But the bad ones were all he could picture right then.

He wove his way through the group, smelling beer on their breaths and stale cigarettes on their clothes, and his gut tightened.

"Gracie!"

He scanned the sidewalk across the street, picking up his pace. Surely she wouldn't have crossed the road—she *definitely* knew not to do that. She was always good about waiting to hold his hand before stepping off the sidewalk.

"Gracie!" he called. Louder this time.

A few people looked over at him, but he barely noticed. He knew there was an edge of fear to his voice, but he barely noticed that either.

"Ben."

Turning, he saw Kyla walking toward him. Gracie was holding her hand, and waved happily.

His heartbeat slowed, and he let out a long breath. *Thank sweet baby Jesus.* She'd definitely be getting a lecture for this. One of his longer-winded ones that always made her squirm in her seat, which was probably punishment enough for anyone.

"I'm so sorry," Kyla said, letting go of Gracie's hand and watching as she ran up to him. "She came into the shop to see Jacques, and I didn't realize you were so far behind. You must've been worried sick."

He looked at her gratefully. Then kneeled on one knee and took Gracie's shoulders in both hands. "You never *ever* run off like that again, do you understand me?"

Her dark eyes widened. He was scaring her.

Pulling her into a hug, he patted her back when she started to cry. After a few seconds, he took her by the shoulders again, this time gentler.

"It was okay this time, honey, because Kyla was here to bring you back. But what if it was somebody who wasn't so nice? Remember what I've told you about talking to strangers? About getting out of my sight?"

Tears streamed down Gracie's cheeks, breaking his heart into a thousand pieces.

"But Kyla isn't a stranger," she said, "and I just wanted to see Jacques really quick because Frances said it was his birthday this week, and we haven't even gotten him a present yet."

"I know she's not a stranger, but you were away from me and there were strangers all around you.

You can't just go running off like that. Ever. I don't care whose birthday it is—got it?"

She nodded.

"I just love you so much," he said, his voice low. "And I can't protect you if I can't see you."

Sniffing, she nodded again. The tears had stopped, thank God. Kids were resilient. In a minute, she'd be eating ice cream, having forgotten all about it. He was the one who'd be reliving this moment over and over again, ad nauseam.

He stood up, letting his gaze settle on Kyla. "Thank you," he said. "For bringing her back. It was only a minute or two, but when you can't find your kid…"

"You don't have to explain. You're a good dad."

"Can Kyla come for ice cream with us, Daddy?"

"Oh…" Kyla said. "I don't want to butt in."

She looked lovely tonight in jeans and a simple white T-shirt. It was thin enough to see a hint of a lacy bra underneath, outlining the soft swell of her breasts.

His throat went suddenly dry, but Gracie tugged on his hand, pulling him away from the dangerous thoughts he was leaning toward. The problem was, he knew exactly how Kyla's body felt pressed against his. It was no longer just a concept in his imagination. And that made it a lot harder to keep his gaze locked firmly on hers, where it absolutely belonged.

"Daddy?"

"What about the shop?" he asked Kyla.

She shrugged, her eyes sparkling. "We're closing up. And I do like ice cream." She winked at Gracie, who appeared ready to pop from anticipation.

Actually, despite his stupid speech from the other night, about how he couldn't let Gracie get attached, and blah, blah, blah, he was finding that all he wanted to do was let her have what she wanted. Which was Kyla. Even if it was only for a few precious minutes, because she was exactly what he wanted, too.

He guessed he had his sister to thank for this. Maybe he going to leave the door open a crack after all.

He smiled down at Gracie. "Well, what are we waiting for? Let's hit it."

Kyla walked beside Ben, licking her ice-cream cone in the dusky evening light, and watching Gracie chase some other little girls around the jungle gym in the distance. Holmes Park was only a few blocks over from Main Street, and had a nice walking path that circled the playground, so parents could keep an eye on their kids while getting some exercise of their own. After Ben's scare earlier, Kyla thought it was a genius design. Score one for multitasking Christmas Bay moms and dads.

Ben leaned across her and tossed his napkin in a garbage can as they passed. He'd finished his ice cream five minutes ago. A double scoop that looked like it had about a gazillion calories in it.

Her own tasted so good that it curled her toes inside her ballet flats. Or maybe that had everything to do with the man beside her.

Licking some chocolate from her lips, she glanced over at him now. He was so good-looking. Better looking than any man had a right to be. But the thing about Ben was that he didn't seem to be aware of it. Or, if he was, he didn't really care that much. The effect was devastating. She had to wonder how many women had lost their hearts to Ben Martinez since high school. Probably plenty.

He looked over at her and smiled. "Is it good?"

For a second she couldn't understand what he was talking about. The ice cream, or the view. "Oh," she finally said. "Very good. Rich."

"Best ice cream around. Rivaled only by the candy shop down the street."

"I don't know about that, but the gummy worms are poppin'. That's how Hunter puts it, anyway."

"I know a little girl who's a veritable gummy worm expert, and she agrees. Maybe not in those exact words, but whatever."

She laughed. "A five-star review. We'll take it."

They continued walking as she finished the last of her cone, then dabbed her napkin over her mouth. She hadn't had dinner yet, and she could almost feel the sugar coursing through her veins. She'd forgotten how happy a summer stroll with an ice-cream cone made her. She'd forgotten how happy a lot of things made her.

"You know," Ben said. "I haven't been able to stop thinking about you since the other night."

Her stomach dipped. So, he was going to talk about it. They weren't just about to ignore it and hope it went away. It was the mature thing to do. Still, Kyla stuck her hands in her pockets and looked down at her feet. Talking about it was mature, but that didn't mean it would be easy. Mostly because it was getting harder and harder to hide how she felt about Ben. And harder and harder to deny it to herself.

He slowed. Then touched her arm before coming to a stop.

"Hey."

She stopped too, feeling her heart crack open like a book without her consent.

"I'm having a hard time with this, Kyla," he said. "And I meant what I said about it being a bad idea, you and me. But everything that comes out of my mouth lately seems like a damn contradiction."

She looked up at him. His eyes were so deep and warm. She thought about his ex-wife, and wondered how anyone could walk away from Ben, when all she wanted to do was walk toward him. To be wrapped in his arms, and feel safe and secure. How could anyone walk away from that?

Yet, she felt herself fighting, fighting. Like she always did when her wants and desires got too close to the surface. Because what would happen if she let herself want something, or worse, need it, and then it was taken away? Kyla was a fighter. She didn't know how to be anything else. The question was, could she ever stop fighting long enough to find some peace.

"I guess I just wanted you to know that," Ben finished quietly. "That kiss meant something to me."

She felt herself melting inside. He was like a flame licking at her frosty heart. It was coming to life by the second, beating with a ferocity that made her knees weak. Was this what losing yourself to someone felt like? This heat and desire, excitement and fear, all rolled into one? She guessed it probably was. She'd never loved anyone else but Ben.

"It meant something to me, too," she said, her voice hoarse. It was hard to be honest like this. But it was also hard not to follow his lead. She was acutely aware that he was teaching her how to face life, when life came at you swinging.

They watched each other, the kids' laughter ringing like a bell across the park. Stars were beginning to twinkle overhead now, scattered across the heavens like sugar. How sweet it was to be standing underneath them, feeling the delicacy of the nighttime air against her cheeks. The wonder of the spinning world beneath her feet.

Before she realized it, and maybe before he even realized it, he bent close. And for the second time in a matter of days, she allowed herself to be pulled into his orbit. She breathed in his scent, so uniquely him. She took comfort in his warmth, in his solidness. And she pushed every other thought away, as he leaned in and kissed her.

He'd been gentle before, but this time she could feel an urgency in his touch. She wanted more of it, more of him, until she heard herself make a soft sound when he pulled away. A sound of longing, of frustration. She'd been given another glimpse, but only a glimpse. What lay beyond was a mystery she could only guess at.

"Gracie," he murmured. "She'll see, and I'm not sure I'd know what to say to her yet..."

Kyla felt a pang of guilt. The thought of Gracie hadn't even occurred to her.

Looking toward the playground, she spotted her immediately in her bright pink shirt and matching shoes. She hadn't seen. She was climbing up the ladder to the slide, gloriously lost in the magic of play.

Kyla frowned, knowing how hopeful that little heart was. How much it wanted to love and be loved. She'd been there. There was still a bit of that hopefulness inside her too, although she'd tried hard over the years to bury it deep down.

"Does she miss her mom?" she asked, looking back up at Ben.

His expression tightened. "I think she misses the idea of her mom. I think the memory of Sam is fading some, and that's a blessing. The more abstract Sam is, the less painful she can be for her."

Kyla knew all too well that a memory could be just as vivid as the person if it lodged itself in your brain right. It was probably too early to tell if that was the case with Gracie or not, but she had a feeling it might be. Still, she wasn't going to say that to Ben, who looked like he was struggling with memories of his own.

"The truth is," he said, "I don't know how to give her everything she needs. I do the best I can, but I'm still not her mother. I don't cut her hair right. I don't know what clothes match and what don't." He swallowed, his Adam's apple bobbing up and down. "Sometimes all I can think about is her wedding day. Who's going to be there to help her get ready? I can give her away, but I can't be the one to button up her dress. Those things are what I worry about. The pivotal things in her life. The things she'll miss having a mom for the most."

Kyla felt her throat constrict. She'd dreamed of having a dad as wonderful and loving as Ben when she'd been Gracie's age. And even though she was a grown woman now, she'd still give anything to have a father in her life. But those weren't the cards she'd been dealt. She had Frances. She had Stella and Marley. They were her family. And they would be there for her pivotal things.

"Gracie is a lucky girl," Kyla said. "It might take her a while to understand just how lucky, but trust me, she will. And when her wedding day comes, all she's going to feel is love for her dad, and gratitude for how well he brought her up in this world."

He let that settle, the tight expression softening in a way that made her want to reach up and touch him. To feel that five-o'clock shadow underneath her fingertips.

"Daddy, look!"

They both turned to see Gracie standing at the top of the slide, her arms stretched wide.

"I'm the king of the world!"

"She's going through a *Titanic* phase," Ben said. "She watched it at Isabel's a few weeks ago, and knows the entire thing by heart. Don't ask me how."

Kyla laughed, watching Gracie plop down and slide on her stomach. "She's fearless."

"Tell me about it. Just as long as she doesn't want to reenact the iceberg scene."

"But that's the best part."

"Where they die?"

Looking up at him, she smiled. "Where they find the meaning of life, smart-guy."

"Which is?"

"Love," she said simply. "Just love."

Kyla looked up as a particularly strong gust of wind shook the candy shop's windows. The weather guy had been right a few days ago, predicting the storm's arrival for that afternoon, and the dark, ominous clouds had followed soon after. In the distance, the ocean rocked and rolled, and most of the shops on Main Street were closing up early. Everybody wanted to be safely tucked at home if the power went out.

She looked over at Hunter, who was cleaning the licorice bins so carefully, that he seemed oblivious to the storm building outside. Her heart swelled. As an employee, he was turning out to be a good one. Coming in early, and leaving late—even if sometimes that was because he was busy giving Jacques extra cuddles. The important thing was that he'd proved himself to be reliable and hardworking, and for Kyla, that was all that really mattered.

But today, he seemed different. He was quieter and more withdrawn than he'd been over the last week or so. It was also the first time he'd come in without wearing one of the collared shirts he was so proud of. Today, his trademark hoodie was back, even though the shop was fairly warm this evening. Too warm for a sweatshirt.

She frowned. Something was off, but she didn't know what. And by the look on Frances's face, she felt the same.

Glancing over at Kyla briefly, Frances picked up the keys and handed them to Hunter.

"Here, honey. Why don't you go ahead and lock up? I don't think anyone's going to be interested in candy with weather coming in like it is."

He nodded, gave her a small smile, and did as he was told. The wind howled outside, sending the flower baskets underneath the awning, swinging wildly. A woman ran down the sidewalk, holding her skirt down with both hands.

But Kyla kept her gaze settled on Hunter. He'd definitely turned out to be a good employee. But he was also a sweet kid, whom she and Frances had genuinely come to care about. And try as she might, she couldn't ignore the funny feeling in her stomach at the sight of him locking the door now. At the way his shoulders were slumped. At that sweatshirt, so out of place, that it felt like some kind of warning flag to her.

Steeling herself, she stepped out from behind the counter, and walked toward him. Not really knowing what she was going to say, but knowing she didn't want him to leave tonight without at least asking if he was okay. If things were alright at home. If he needed anything. She'd have to word it delicately, she knew by now that he'd shut down if she was too forward, but she had to make a decent attempt to reach him.

"Hunter…" she began softly.

He turned, his eyebrows raised. He had a fresh pimple on his chin that looked sore. There was downy peach fuzz on his top lip, and his newly trimmed hair was brushed back, and out of his eyes for once. He had nice, expressive eyes. But at the moment, there was hesitation in them. Almost like he suspected what she was about to say.

She reached out and touched his elbow. "I just wanted to make sure everything is okay? You've been pretty quiet."

Looking down at the floor, he nodded. "Yeah. Yeah, I'm okay."

She shouldn't push. She knew that from her own experience, but it was hard not to. He seemed almost fragile tonight. Like the slightest touch might make him crack into a million pieces.

"But you would tell us?" she said. "If there was something wrong?"

He didn't answer. After a few seconds, he took a shallow breath. "I'd better get home. My mom will worry if I'm out too late in this."

He held the keys out to her, and she felt a distinct heaviness settle in her chest. So, he was going to ignore that. It was possible she wouldn't be able to reach him at all. No matter how hard she tried. No matter how much she pushed.

She looked down at the keys in his hand. His sweatshirt sleeve had ridden up a little. Not a lot. But enough that her pulse slowed. And then everything finally clicked into place. The change in his behavior, his baggie hoodie, the look in his eyes...

Bruises, dark as the clouds that had rolled in on the storm, encircled his wrist.

And her heart broke.

Chapter Eleven

Ben looked at his watch and grabbed Gracie's rainbow suitcase by the front door.

"Gracie, we've got to go!"

"Coming!" she shouted from down the hall. She'd forgotten Henry the Hippo at the last minute. Then she'd needed to go to the bathroom at the last, *last* minute, leaving him standing there trying to keep his patience. At this rate, he'd definitely be late for work, and it was going to be a long night.

He didn't usually work the night shift, but during storms their small department needed all hands on deck. There were going to be strong winds and surf with this one. Lots of people would probably lose power, and no matter how prepared everyone was, widespread power outages usually caused all kinds of trouble.

Anticipating this, he'd asked Isabel to keep Gracie, which she'd been great about, as usual. They were going to paint each other's toenails and watch *Tangled*. Gracie was thrilled. She loved this kind of time with her aunt.

He grabbed his keys from the hook by the door. "Gracie, I'm going to count to five. I'm not kidding."

"I'm coming, Daddy! I just have to wash my hands!"

Sighing, he looked out the window. The wind was whipping the cedar in the yard back and forth, and the rain was coming down in sheets. It wouldn't normally be dark for another hour or so, but the steely gray clouds had gobbled up the sun, and the streetlights had already come on.

He hoped, like he always did during these storms, that the tourists would have enough sense to stay away from the beach during the worst of it. But he also knew that storm watching was one of Christmas Bay's biggest draws. The waves up and down Cape Longing could be spectacular, some of them reaching up to thirty feet or more offshore. Which made for great storm watching, but dangerous conditions for anyone reckless enough to want to get close. He'd seen it too many times to count.

Hearing Gracie clomp down the hall in her rain boots, he turned.

She stood there clutching Henry the Hippo, the hood of her purple slicker hanging down over her eyes.

"Okay," she said. "I'm ready."

"Alright, kiddo. I'll call you later, and see how it's going, okay?"

She nodded. "Are you going to be home in time for pancakes?"

"I'll try. But we'll have to see how it goes. I'm going to be pretty busy."

"Remember when that big old tree fell down in Mrs. Ellis's yard last year?"

He remembered. It had fallen on her house, narrowly missing her bedroom. Just another reminder to be on his toes tonight.

"I do. She had to get a new roof." He touched her chin. "So, you've got everything? Toothbrush? Jammies?"

She gave him a thumbs-up. "Affirmative."

"Alright then. Let's go."

Kyla pulled her hood over her head and turned the flashlight on. The wind howled and whistled around the old house, rain pummeling the gabled roof like miniature knives being thrown from heaven.

It was a miserable night, but she had to find Jacques, who'd bolted out the front door when she'd come home with takeout. This wasn't the first time he'd pulled a stunt like this. The wind always spooked him, and for some reason, he seemed to think he'd be safer outside in the elements, than inside in his cushy bed.

Frances was getting her pajamas on upstairs, which was just as well. She'd had a hard evening, and Kyla didn't want her to worry, which she absolutely would. The cat probably hadn't gone far, anyway. His favorite hiding spot was a little cubbyhole beside the woodshed. Which was great, because it was definitely protected. But that also meant she'd have to cross the yard to get to him, which wasn't so great. She just hoped she wouldn't get blown away in this ridiculous wind.

With a quick look behind her to make sure Frances was still upstairs, she zipped her slicker to her chin, and opened the door. A gust of wind immediately pushed her back, and she put her head down, training the flashlight on the yard ahead. She closed the door behind her and squinted into the stinging rain.

"Jacques! Here, kitty, kitty!"

The chances of him coming in this were slim to none, but it was worth a shot.

"Jacques!"

Taking an even breath, she stepped onto the walkway and shone the flashlight into the pines. They were swaying back and forth like saplings. The waves crashed against the cliffs below, and she could imagine the foam and spray flying a hundred feet into the stormy night air. As a kid, she'd been terrified that the swells would reach the house and pull it back into the ocean with them.

Now she knew she was safe from the water, but definitely not from something falling on her in this wind. Most likely one of the pine trees, which were old and had to fall over sometime. She just hoped it wouldn't be with her trying to find Jacques with nothing but her hood over her head for protection.

She made her way carefully along the picket fence. They'd usually lose a few slats in this kind of weather, but tonight the wood and rusty nails were holding, clinging to each other out of pure survival.

"Jacques!"

The rain pelted her in the face as she struggled to see through the weakening beam of the flashlight. She pounded on it until it flickered back to life, and pointed it in the direction of the woodshed a few yards away. Sure enough, two yellow eyes peered back at her.

"Jacques, you idiot," she said with a groan.

Bending to set the flashlight down, she unzipped her slicker. The cat blinked up at her and gave a hoarse meow as another gust of wind made her plant her feet apart to stay upright.

"You're officially in a time-out, mister."

He meowed again.

"Don't argue."

She reached into his little hole and grabbed him with both hands. He stiffened, and she pulled him out as gently as she could.

"It's okay, buddy," she said. "I know. But we can't leave you out here in this."

She cradled him against her chest, tucking the slicker around him as best she could.

Then picked up the flashlight, and turned toward

the house. But froze when she saw red-and-blue lights flashing through the trees. A police car, making its way up the winding driveway, its lights like a strobe through the darkness and rain.

Clutching the cat, Kyla jogged toward the house. Why in the world would the police be up here at this hour, in this storm? And if they had bad news to deliver, she knew they wouldn't be using their lights. Which meant only one thing.

Frances had called them.

Jacques meowed and struggled briefly against her chest as the wind blew her hood back. The rain immediately soaked her hair, pasting strands of it to her face.

The cruiser came to a stop, its tires skidding in the gravel. The door opened and a young officer stepped out—a woman with her blond hair pulled back into a bun.

"Stop right there!" she yelled over the wind.

Kyla froze, her heart hammering in her chest. "I live here."

"We got a call about an intruder. What's your name?"

"Kyla Beckett."

"Just stay right there." The officer watched Kyla through the rain, and cued the mic on her shoulder. Probably confirming this with Dispatch. After a second, she seemed to relax a little and dropped her hand to her side.

"What's in your jacket?"

"Our cat," Kyla said, opening her slicker enough for her to see. "He got out."

The officer nodded. "Let's get you inside."

She didn't argue with that. The rain was dripping down her neck and had soaked the back of her sweater underneath the slicker. Jacques struggled some more, and one of his claws scraped her belly, making her wince.

She made her way to the front door, where Frances now stood holding her hand over her mouth.

"Kyla?" she managed.

"It's okay, Frances. It was just me. Jacques got out."

Kyla stepped inside the foyer and plopped a sopping Jacques down on the floor. He shook himself, and then stalked off stiff legged.

The officer stepped inside too, making sure to wipe her chunky black boots on the welcome mat first.

"Looks like this was just a misunderstanding, then?" she asked.

Kyla glanced over at Frances, who seemed embarrassed.

"That's right. It was dark, and Frances didn't know I was outside."

Frances walked slowly into the kitchen, and sat down at the table, her shoulders slumped.

The officer's radio crackled, and the dispatcher said something about a tree down by the library. It was blocking part of the road.

Turning the volume down, the officer smiled,

looking tired. "Well, if things are okay here, I've got another call."

"Of course," Kyla said. "We're alright."

"Just stay inside if you can. It's supposed to get worse before it gets better, and the biggest dangers are downed trees and power lines."

"We'll stay inside," Kyla said. "Thank you so much."

"Yes, thank you," Frances said. "Stay safe."

The officer opened the door against the storm, and closed it quickly again behind her.

After locking the dead bolt, Kyla headed straight to the teapot and turned the burner on. Then peeled her soggy sweater off, leaving her tank top on underneath.

"Good God," Frances said, putting her head in her hands. "She thought this was some kind of home invasion because of me. You could've been shot."

"Don't be silly, Frances. It's fine."

"But it's not fine. It's not fine at all."

"Well, I should've told you I was going outside," Kyla said, draping her sweater over the back of a chair. "This could've happened to anyone."

That was absolutely true. It could've happened to anyone. But as soon as she said it, she knew this level of fear and confusion went beyond just thinking someone had been in the yard. Frances was legitimately shaken. She'd already been upset when they'd closed the shop for the night, and now she was practically beside herself.

When the little teapot began to whistle, Kyla took it off the burner and grabbed a teacup from the cabinet. She put a tea bag in, filled it with steaming water and set it down in front of her foster mother.

"Here," she said. "Peppermint. Your favorite."

The wind rattled the single-paned windows, making Kyla say a prayer nothing would break. Then, after a second, she pulled out a chair and sat down. "Do you want to talk about it?" she asked.

"What's the point?"

But Kyla knew the answer to that. Healthy communication would help them move forward. And talking about it, even when Frances didn't want to, would probably make her feel better. At least a little.

Frances looked up, her blue eyes sad. "I don't know what's happening to me. I feel like an old woman practically overnight. I feel like I'm in this fog all the time, and I'm sure people can see it. I'm sure they notice. It's humiliating."

Her voice hitched when she said this, and it broke Kyla's heart. She knew she was embarrassed. She knew she was scared. But she wasn't going to have to face this alone. Any of it.

Kyla took her hand. Her skin was so soft, so delicate. Frances had always taken pride in her skin, putting all kinds of creams and lotions on before bed. The girls used to tease her about it when she'd come in to say good-night with her face glistening, and her hands smelling like a thousand coconuts. But whatever she'd done had worked. She was still as luminous in her sixties as she'd been in her forties. Maybe with a few more wrinkles around her eyes, but still so pretty, that sometimes it took Kyla's breath away.

"People here are your friends," Kyla said. "They love you. And remember what you told me in the eighth grade when Tiffany Rhodes teased me for being skinny?"

Frances gave her a small smile.

"You told me she could sit and spin."

"Well. That sounds like me."

Kyla squeezed her fingers. "I know Christmas Bay is a small town, and I know people talk. But they're always going to talk. The ones who matter, the ones who love you, and there are a *lot* of them who do, are the ones who matter."

"You're so good to me, honey. Such a good girl."

"I just care about you, Frances. It's going to be okay."

Her foster mother's gaze fell to the teacup in front of her. She looked skeptical. "What am I going to do?" she asked softly.

Kyla scooted close to give her a hug. Then leaned back to look her in the eyes. "I think we just need a plan," she said. "Having some kind of plan for the future will alleviate a lot of stress for you. I know it would make me feel better. And Stella and Marley, too."

Frances glanced up sharply. "You've talked to them?"

Kyla nodded, still holding Frances's gaze. "I talked

to Marley the other day. She's planning on coming back to Christmas Bay pretty soon. Maybe to stay. She's looking for a job."

"You see? I never wanted this. For you three to be having to take care of me like this."

Frances was clearly frustrated now. A little angry. Kyla braced herself for it. There would be a lot of emotion in the months to come. Maybe in the years to come. It wouldn't be easy. In fact, navigating this together might be the hardest thing any of them would ever do.

"I know you didn't," Kyla said evenly. "But sometimes life is messy. What choice do we have?"

After a minute, Frances took a long sip of tea, then set the cup down to rub her eyes. "It was just a hard night," she said. "And I've noticed that if I'm worried about something, or stressed about something, my memory or just my state of mind is foggier. It's not just anxiety—it feels different. Like the balance between my emotions is more delicate. I get mad easier, scared easier." She looked up at Kyla. "So, when I saw the flashlight in the yard tonight, and I called for you and you weren't in the house, I just went straight to terrified. No thinking it through, none of that. Just terrified."

Kyla reached for her hand again. Being able to stay calm in a crisis had always been one of Frances's superpowers. Once, Stella had fallen off her scooter and broken her arm. Kyla remembered rushing over to her, and seeing her elbow bent at an odd angle. She'd looked up at her foster mother in a panic. Frances had just told her to get in the car, they were going to the hospital. Kyla remembered it like it was yesterday—that evenness to her voice, the reassuring look in her eyes. She'd been so *strong*.

Sitting here now, holding her foster mother's hand, Kyla knew it was time for her to be the strong one. If Frances wasn't going to be able to lead them through this like she'd led them through everything else, they would have to turn the tables. They would have to be brave for her.

Frances took another sip of tea. In the corner, Jacques was busy licking himself. He looked like a drowned rat, his black-and-white fur sticking up in tufts all over his body. The rain continued lashing at the windows, and for a second the lights flickered, bringing the shadows in the old house closer.

Kyla looked up. Probably time to get the candles out.

"What are we going to do?" Frances asked, her voice low.

"There's a fresh flashlight in the cupboard. And the candles you bought last spring. That should hold us for the night."

"No. I'm not talking about the power, honey."

Kyla frowned. And then the realization set in. Her stomach, which had been punchy ever since the police officer had shown up, now twisted almost painfully. Frances wasn't talking about the power, and she wasn't talking about her dementia.

Putting her elbows on the table, Kyla took a deep breath. "About Hunter…"

Frances nodded. They hadn't talked about him since they'd closed the shop that evening. Since they'd driven home alongside the turbulent sea. And since they'd walked through the doors of the old Victorian, its walls creaking against the assault of the storm.

But his name was out now, and hanging in the air between them, while Frances cradled her teacup in her hands and Kyla felt a shiver move up her spine that had nothing to do with the dampness of the night.

What are we going to do?

Slowly, she sat back in her chair, and listened to the wind howling through the pines outside. It was a complicated question, because once upon a time, she'd been on the other side of it. She'd been the one whose future hung in the balance after someone else's information had come to light. She understood very clearly what direction this could take, how devastating it could end up being. And it did more than turn her stomach. It made her want to run away, as far and as fast as she possibly could. *Fight or flight…*

But the problem was, she was now an adult who couldn't run away when things got hard. She couldn't just leave Christmas Bay and start new somewhere else. She had people who needed her here. Responsibilities to them, and to her community. But the question was still as simple as Frances had put it a minute ago. And still just as raw. *What are we going to do?*

She shook her head. "I don't know, Frances," she said. "I really don't."

Chapter Twelve

Ben eased the cruiser along the steep dirt drive, keeping an eye on the trees overhead. They whipped back and forth, sending pine needles raining down on his roof.

Leaning forward, he looked up at the big house on the cliff. Its characteristically warm, light-filled windows were completely dark now, its hulk on the mountainside looking still and ominous. It had been that way for the last half an hour.

If you were in the right spot in town, like the gas station on the corner, or the library parking lot, you could see the house in the distance. Out of habit tonight, or maybe because he'd been thinking about Kyla nonstop, he'd glanced up at it when he'd gotten the call to assist for the downed tree. The darkened windows meant they'd lost power. And no power, even in this day and age, could be dangerous if the circumstances were right.

He eased over a pothole now, then stepped on the gas, feeling the car's tires spin underneath him. He'd been out with a stranded motorist earlier when he'd heard the intruder call over the radio. It had been all he could do to stay with the poor lady while one of his officers checked it out. Thank God it had turned out to be nothing, but Frances and Kyla were probably shaken. And now they were sitting up there in the dark, not answering their damn phone, which was going straight to voice mail. Which meant he wasn't going to relax until he'd checked on them himself.

He turned the cruiser sharply to the left and through the trees, and the house came into view again. From this close he could see the softest light burning in the windows—candles, the flames of which danced in the darkness.

Feeling the knot in his stomach ease a little, he pulled up and cut the engine. Then cued the mic on his shoulder.

"Forty-seven twenty-one."

"Forty-seven twenty-one," the dispatcher replied. "Go ahead."

"Out at eight sixty-three Old Mariner's Lane. Follow-up."

"Eight sixty-three Old Mariner's Lane. Copy that."

Ben opened the door into the wind and rain, hunching his shoulders against the onslaught. Then jogged toward the front door with his jacket collar pulled high around his neck.

He gave three firm knocks and waited. After a second, the door opened with a creak.

"Ben?" Kyla stood there holding a candle, shadows flickering across her pretty face. "What's wrong?"

"Nothing. I just saw from down the road that you'd lost power up here. And I heard the call earlier. I wanted to check on you, make sure you were okay."

She smiled, her eyes looking darker than he'd ever seen them. Tonight, they were slate gray. Her skin was pale in the candlelight. Delicate, almost translucent. She stepped aside.

"Can you come in for a minute? It's miserable out there."

Honestly, the pull of her gaze was just as tempting as the chance to get warm and dry for a few minutes. The word *miserable* didn't do this night justice.

Nodding, he stepped past her and into the foyer. There was a fire crackling in the hearth, and the smell of woodsmoke filled his senses. The logs shifted, sending sparks rising like stars into the chimney. There were a few candles burning in the living room, and their warm yellow light danced over the walls.

Ben felt something brush against his legs, and looked down to see Jacques wind himself around his boots. The cat gazed up at him and meowed. He looked a little rough around the edges.

"Is he wet?"

Kyla set her candle on a shelf by the front door. "He's wet and then some. You wouldn't believe the night we've had so far."

Ben turned to her, scrubbing a hand through his hair. "Tell me about it." He looked around. "Where's Frances?"

"She went to bed. She was exhausted. Physically, emotionally..."

He frowned, watching her pull her oversize cardigan around her shoulders. It was obvious that her hair had been soaked recently. It was wild, hanging next to her face in damp waves.

She smiled up at him. "Honestly, I'm just happy to see you."

"Oh, yeah?"

Her eyes filled with sudden tears.

"Hey, hey," he said, reaching out to pull her close. "What's wrong?"

His uniform jacket was beaded with rain, but she didn't seem to care. It was like she'd been waiting for the contact, and relaxed into him with a soft sigh.

"Everything," she said against his chest. "Everything's wrong."

He cupped the back of her head in his hand, and bent to kiss the crown, smelling her shampoo, the scent of rain. Desire stirred in his gut. Would there ever come a time when he wouldn't want to watch over her anymore? It seemed like with every passing day, that need only grew more pronounced inside him.

Sniffing, she pulled away and raised her chin. Just a little, but that toughness he'd come to know so well was evident in the tilt of her head. He knew Kyla was used to taking care of herself. But it was also clear that she'd wanted his arms around her just then. She was a walking contradiction. Someone whose pain would probably always dictate how close she let people get. It would take a strong man to gain her trust, a man whose own pain wouldn't get in the way.

At that, he licked his lips. His mouth felt dry as he stood there looking down at her. Her sweater had slipped off one milky shoulder, and he wanted to lean down and put his mouth there. To taste her, and feel her skin under his lips.

She was so beautiful, but he was acutely aware that her beauty wasn't all that was drawing him to her at that moment. It was the way she was watching him. There was almost a challenge in her eyes, whether she realized it or not. *Are you strong enough?*

"What is it, Kyla?" he asked. "What's going on?"

Clasping her hands in front of her belly, she took a deep breath. "It's Hunter."

"Oh shit."

"No, it's not what you think."

He waited, skeptical.

She looked toward the windows as a gust of wind rattled the house. Then shifted her gaze back to his.

"He was stocking the shelves today," she began quietly. "He'd just gotten done telling us about a fight he had with his dad a few nights ago. I guess he's not happy Hunter's working at Coastal Sweets, even though he'd originally said it was okay."

Ben's chest tightened. He'd been worried about this.

"Frances and I just listened," she went on. "I was afraid if I said too much, he'd clam up, and it was obvious he needed to talk about it. Who knows if he's got friends he can confide in? He seems close with his mom, and it seems like she's doing the best she can, but she's also walking on eggshells around this guy."

Ben knew that was putting it mildly. She was probably afraid of him. Maybe even wanted to leave him, but was scared to. It was possible. Anything was possible.

"So," she said, "he told us this story about how his dad came into his room and started yelling and throwing things. But that he eventually calmed down, and everything was okay." She shook her head. "It felt like he was glossing it over, though. You can tell when people do that. They're protecting something. Or someone."

His heartbeat slowed, as he remembered Kyla as a little kid. Remembered when she'd come over to his parents' house for those Sunday dinners, she'd do the same thing. She wasn't that hungry, she'd say. She wasn't that tired. Her jeans fit, she just needed a belt. And when she'd talk about her mother, her posture would change—it would stiffen like she was getting ready for a fight. She'd never say a word against her mom. Not once in all the time he'd known her. He'd had to look past those walls to see the truth.

She chewed her cheek for a minute. "We knew he was hiding something," she finally said. "And I'm not surprised, because he loves working at the shop. He doesn't want anything ruining this for him. It was never Hunter we had to worry about trusting. It was his dad. You told us that."

He nodded.

"I was just expecting him to steal something, you know? I never expected to like him so much. And I never thought…"

At that, she stopped, her voice growing strained.

"You never thought what?"

She gazed up at him, and there was something in her expression that unsettled him.

"He was wearing this big sweatshirt," Kyla said slowly. "I thought it was a little strange, because the shop was kind of stuffy tonight. I was only in a tank top, and Frances was in short sleeves. We'd turned the heat up because of the wind, and then it got kind of warm. But he kept his sweatshirt on the entire time. And then he locked up for us, and handed the keys back, and his sleeve slid back."

She swallowed visibly.

"What?" he asked. Wanting to know, but not wanting to know. He had too much experience with this kind of thing to have anything but a sick feeling at the look on her face.

"Bruises," she finished. "Black-and-blue, like a bracelet around his wrist."

"Dammit to hell," he muttered.

"As soon as he realized that we saw, he pulled his sleeve down and said something about falling on his skateboard." She frowned. "He got so upset. We asked him if that's what really happened, and he started crying. I just hugged him. That was all I could do. I just held him until he calmed down."

Ben felt a rush of fury at Gabe Mohatt. It was true they didn't know if he'd given Hunter those bruises or not, but it was a puzzle that wasn't hard to put together if you were paying attention.

"His dad sounds volatile," she said, eyeing him closely, "but do you think he did this?"

"I don't know, but I'm going to find out."

"Yes, of course. But how can we say something without Hunter's blessing first? He could be taken away. And he's close with this mother…or seems to be."

Ben stared at her, but bit his tongue. What he wanted to say was how *couldn't* they say something? It was the same question that had haunted him as a teenager. And the answer was, he'd had to say something because Kyla's safety had been on the line.

It was possible that just because Hunter was older than she'd been, or that he had one parent who actually seemed to care about him, she wasn't ready to go there. Or maybe it was simply that she'd lived through being taken away herself, and knew how it felt.

She shook her head. "It's too early."

"Kyla, he could be in real trouble, and we're mandatory reporters. The choice isn't ours to make."

Crossing her arms over her chest, she turned away from him. "I know that. I know it's our responsibility to say something, and I will. Of course I will. I just want more time. To make sure. To prepare him."

"Kyla…"

She turned back, her eyes flashing in the candlelight. "He needs time, Ben. Nobody gave me any time."

He knew what she meant by that. *He* never gave her any time. He was so sorry she'd been hurt, but reporting her situation was something he couldn't be sorry for. He'd done what he thought was right at the time, and he'd do it again.

"No," he said, his voice sharp. "But it was because you were taken away when you were that you didn't have to see your mom—"

She glared up at him, and it was the first time since the day Hunter took the tip jar that she'd looked at him like this. With such naked hostility.

"That I didn't have to see my mom, what?" she said coolly.

"Hey. We're both on the same side, here."

"No," she said, ignoring that. "I didn't have to see my mom die. You're right. But maybe it was *because* I was taken away that she died. Maybe it was because I wasn't there to help her."

"And you blame me for that."

She continued staring up at him, but didn't say a word. Just looked like she wanted to push him in front of a bus.

"It's okay," he said, anger starting to warm his blood. Or maybe it was a long-buried defensiveness that was only now coming to the surface. "Just be honest for once. You still blame me. You've always blamed me. Let's just have this out now before things go any further."

"Before *what* goes any further? You and me?"

She said this with such disdain that it was like an ice pick to his heart. He had to work not to show how much it stung.

"Yes," he said evenly.

"I'm done talking about this."

"We haven't even started talking about it."

She narrowed her gorgeous eyes at him. "I want you to leave."

"Why? Because I care enough not to let it go? Let me guess—everyone else in your life just bends to your will, am I right? And if they don't…" He snapped his fingers. "You just cut them right the hell out."

"You know nothing about me, Ben."

"I know enough. I know this thing with Hunter scares you, because you might have to face what happened to you as a kid. And you're not used to facing things. You're used to running away from them."

She yanked open the front door and the wind immediately gusted through the entryway.

"Leave," she said.

"I'll go," he countered. "But not until you hear me out." He reached out and closed the door, making sure to do it quietly, so he wouldn't wake Frances.

She gaped up at him. "You've got a lot of nerve, Ben Martinez," she said. "How dare you stand here and lecture me?"

"And how dare you hold something over my head that I did when I was seventeen years old? Something I did to save your *life*?"

"I was just fine before you came along." But she said this with an unmistakable tremble in her voice. Because it was a lie.

She was so used to acting so damn tough all the time. So damn independent. He wondered what would happen if she just gave in for once in her life, and let someone love her? Really love her? But that would require him to drop his idiotic baggage too, and he wasn't sure how to do that yet. Maybe he'd never know how to do it. The thought was enough to make him want to fall to his knees in front of her. To wrap his arms around her waist and beg her to teach him.

Instead, he took a step toward her, and she pursed her lips.

"Why in God's name won't you just let people help you?" he said.

"I don't need your help."

"But you did. You needed someone to step in back then, Kyla. And you know what? Every day, I'm thankful I made that decision, and you know why?

Because you're here right now. You're here looking at me like you hate me, and that's okay, because you made it out. Your mom didn't, and I'm sorry. I really am. But she didn't take you with her, and I'm always going to be thankful for that. No matter how much you hate me for it."

She let out a ragged breath then, choking on a sob. "I hate her," she said. She put her face in her hands. "I hate her for leaving me. I—"

He didn't let her finish. Instead, he reached out and pulled her close. She sobbed in earnest against his chest, great heaving sobs that shook her entire body.

"Shhh," he whispered against her ear. "It's okay, baby. You're going to get through this—I promise you."

She flinched at that. And then he felt her stiffen against him, as if her muscles were rebelling at the words.

Slowly, she put her hands on his chest and pushed away. She took a shaky breath and gazed up at him. Her cheeks were wet, but the tears had stopped.

"How am I going to get through it, Ben?" she asked quietly. "Because I love her and I hate her at the same time. I don't know how to do both, and it's killing me inside."

He looked down at her, wishing with all his heart that he could fix this. But that had always been his problem. He always thought he could fix everything for everyone—Kyla, Gracie, Sam… Sometimes people were just going to hurt. And sometimes they were just going to leave, and there wasn't a damn thing he could do about it, but watch them go.

"I want to be at peace with what happened to me," she continued. "Because, you're right. My life turned out very differently than it would have. But it's the what-ifs that bother me so much. And being with you…"

She faltered on that last word. *You.* Like it meant something, or he meant something, that she wasn't comfortable with. He could relate. He'd been struggling with what Kyla meant to him for weeks now.

"If you care about me," she said, looking over at the fire as the rain pelted the windows outside. "You'll leave now."

His heartbeat slowed in his chest. Despite all their time together, and despite how he felt like she was getting close, she really wasn't ready to forgive him. She might not ever be ready. And he wasn't going to trust her with anything other than a few heated kisses if she wouldn't let down her walls. And *that* was reality.

He stepped around her without another word. If this was what she wanted, he'd give it to her. Because he had nothing else to give.

Opening the door into the wind and rain, he hunched his shoulders and made his way to his cruiser in the darkness.

And heard the door click shut behind him.

* * *

Kyla watched the lights from Ben's car grow faint through the trees, and then disappear altogether.

Slowly, she took her hand away from the curtain and let it fall back into place. She felt numb, like her hand wasn't even attached to her arm. She wiggled her fingers to make sure she wasn't having some kind of stroke, because she'd never felt so detached in her life.

She made her way to the couch and sat down, resting her elbows on her knees. It wasn't that she didn't understand what was happening to her emotionally— she did. Frances had made sure she had counseling as a child, and she'd continued it periodically as an adult. The numbness was a defense mechanism. It was a way to get by. Like Ben had said, only this obviously wasn't what he'd meant. He'd meant she would eventually heal. *She* felt like she'd just get so used to being numb that she'd eventually feel nothing at all.

She looked over at the fire. It was dying down now, its embers glowing a quiet orange. Pretty soon this storm would be over. But it always seemed like there was another one waiting in the wings. That was Christmas Bay for you.

Leaning back, she picked up a throw pillow and hugged it to her chest. She hadn't been prepared for how letting Ben back into her life would turn it upside down. She'd been even less prepared for Hunter, who, through no fault of his own, had dredged up her own screwed-up childhood.

The thought of reporting his bruises made her physically sick. She knew how this would play out. She knew how painful it would be for him. So painful that he might never get over it. But she also knew the reality...

She chewed the inside of her cheek methodically. No matter how hard it would be, she was going to have to push her own trauma aside, and make that phone call. She didn't need time, and she didn't need proof. The law was very clear on this, and it was clear to protect children. Suspicion was enough. Ben was absolutely right—she needed to do it right away. Maybe nothing would come of it. Maybe Hunter really did fall, but someone needed to make sure. He might never forgive Kyla, but at least he'd be safe, and that was the kindest thing she could do for him.

At that particular thought, there was a tickle in her subconscious. And then it was more than a tickle. It was a slowly forming fact that made her shift on the couch. Reporting Hunter's bruises would be the kindest thing she could do for him. Just like Ben reporting her neglect had been the kindest thing he could do for her.

She stared at the fireplace, losing herself in that notion. A notion that for most people would probably be the most obvious thing in the world. But that was the thing about trauma. It blinded you to the obvious.

Kyla pinched the corners of the pillow between

her fingers. What else was right there in front of her face? The fact that she should finally forgive and forget? That would be the healthiest thing. But that would also mean changing the course of her life and how she'd been living it up to this point. Realizing she should forgive was different than actually doing it. Because that would mean letting go of everything that had been protecting her until now, and that was simply too tall of an order. Too much to ask. And Lord help her, she didn't think she was strong enough.

The truth was, Ben had been slowly chipping away at her defenses since she'd come back home. She wanted to love him. But more than that, she wanted to trust him, and to trust herself with that feeling. And that scared her.

She shook her head at the fire that was so completely indifferent to her problems. *No.* No, in order to get right again, in order to straighten all of this out in her heart, she needed to be away from this town and all its associated pain. That didn't mean abandoning Frances. She'd help her figure out her future, and she'd still be close—close enough to see her nearly every day. But not close enough to run into Ben Martinez and be tempted to give all of herself over to him. She'd worked too hard over the years to keep something like that from happening.

She swallowed with some difficulty. No matter what Ben said, no matter what he thought, this wouldn't be running away. It was simply self-preservation. He knew all about that, since he'd been hurt, too.

But as she watched the last of the embers in the fireplace flicker and die, she knew that wasn't true at all. She would be running away.

Again.

Chapter Thirteen

"But why not?"

Gracie had kicked her covers off, and was now gazing up at Ben, her eyes glazed with fever.

He pressed his palm to her forehead. She was still pretty hot, but the Tylenol should be kicking in any time now. If not, he'd be putting her in a cool bath, just like Isabel had said. She'd also told him that anything over 103, and it was time to go to urgent care. All instructions that he was trying to keep straight, while also trying to keep her from getting out of bed for the tenth time that hour.

"Because, honey," he said. "I already told you. No more playdates like that. It's complicated. And besides, I think Kyla is mad at me anyway."

"Why?" Gracie asked, her brows furrowed together. She looked so pathetic with her neon-pink cheeks and damp hair. Dark tendrils of it were stuck to her forehead like spaghetti. Poor kid. Isabel said a virus was going around, and that Joe had just gotten over it. Since Gracie had been at their house during the storm last week, the timing was just about right.

Ben looked at his watch. He'd give it another fifteen minutes, and then it was bath time.

"Because we had a little fight," he said.

"But not a big one."

"No, not a big one."

"What did you fight over?"

"Grown-up stuff."

"Just say you're sorry."

"It's not that easy, pumpkin."

"Sure it is. You say you're sorry, and she won't be mad anymore, and she can come over for more pizza and to finish watching *Frozen*. We never got to finish it last time."

He briefly considered just lying to her. Telling her that he'd ask Kyla over, and then making something up when the time came. But he didn't want to lie to Gracie. Especially about this. She'd been deceived plenty already, and even though this was a small thing in comparison to her mother leaving, he knew it wasn't small in her heart. She was starting to love Kyla. And she deserved the truth.

"Gracie," he said, tucking Henry the Hippo underneath her armpit. "Frances told me that Kyla is probably going to be moving away when school starts. I could say I'm sorry, and we could make up and be friends again, but that doesn't change the fact that she's going to be leaving. I don't want you feeling too sad when she goes, and the more playdates you have, the sadder you'll be."

Gracie's eyes filled with tears. "I don't want her to go. She gives me worms and lets me braid her hair."

He sighed. The truth was, it didn't matter how much he tried to prepare Gracie. Kyla's leaving was going to hurt them both like a son of a bitch anyway. It already did. When she'd told him to leave the other night, it was like a light had gone out in her eyes. She was already gone.

The tears slid down Gracie's hot little cheeks, and he knew this wasn't just the fever, or the fact that she was an only child and usually got what she wanted. This was genuine pain, genuine disappointment. This was what he'd been trying to shield her from the whole time. He'd been so damn stupid. Life was going to happen to his daughter, whether he was standing there trying to fight it back with a sword, or not.

He brushed her cheeks with the backs of his knuckles before the tears made their way into her ears.

"I'm sorry, kiddo." And it wasn't just Kyla he was talking about. It was all of it. She would grow, and his heart would grow with her, and they'd simply have to roll with the punches. But that was a hard concept to swallow when you were six.

"Do you think she'll come back?" Gracie asked hopefully.

"I know she'll come back. Frances is here, and she loves Frances very much."

"I thought she might stay because Frances is like her mommy. I'd never want to leave if I had a mommy like Frances. I think I'd live in a house right next door forever."

His gut twisted. "I know. But it's not Kyla's fault, honey. She's sad about so many things, that I think it would be hard for her to stay here."

"Maybe she'll change her mind. Maybe she'll stay…"

It looked like her eyes were getting heavy. She blinked a few times, and then closed them, breathing deeply. Ben felt her forehead again. He thought she was cooler. Not a ton, but a little.

He pulled the sheet up over her legs, and she turned her head into Henry the Hippo with a sigh. He felt some of the tension in his shoulders ease as she slipped into sleep. Hopefully she'd stay comfortable and get a few uninterrupted hours. As for him, he knew he wouldn't sleep a wink.

Easing himself off the bed, he turned off her lamp and walked quietly out of the room. Then headed into the kitchen for something to drink.

He sat down on the couch and looked out the window to the night sky. It was crowded with stars. When his eyes weren't focused on it, the Milky Way looked like a creamy patch against the blackness.

Millions of planets and stars, many of which had died out a long time ago, were still reaching across the heavens to light them up. What a hopeful thought that was.

Ben took a sip of his soda, and thought of his daughter asleep in the next room—maybe snippets of their conversation appearing in her dreams. She wanted to be loved so badly. And when someone like Kyla appeared, and then disappeared like one of those stars, that light was going to linger for a long time.

Setting the can down on the coffee table, he ran a hand through his hair. He'd seen her around town a handful of times since the storm, and every time, she'd been polite, but distant. Which was worse than if she'd just come right up to him and slapped him across the face. He knew that she'd reported Hunter's bruises right away, which he'd known she would once she had a chance to think it through. But it was obvious the whole situation had hit too close to home for her, and he understood that. He got it.

What he'd really wanted to do when he'd seen her coming out of Coastal Sweets yesterday was to kiss her again. To pick up where they'd left off. To see if anything would come of those kisses, like he'd been starting to secretly hope for. But the time for that had come and gone. She'd shifted the other night. She was in a different place now, and it seemed like he was, too. The damaged place. The place he hated, but couldn't seem to shake free of.

He looked out the window again, his thoughts chaotic and heavy. He pictured Hunter, in his hoodie and Converse All Stars, and wondered what, or who, really put those bruises on his arm. Ben had a friend at child protective services, and he knew they were looking into it, but so far had no proof. Hunter wasn't talking, and neither was his mother. Gabe, of course, denied laying a finger on his son, so at the moment, there was nothing but suspicion to go on. Which was enough to report, but wasn't enough for much else.

Ben frowned. He just hoped the kid would be okay. That no matter what happened from here on out, he'd stay on the right path. And that someday, he'd be able to find some peace in his future.

Hopefully Kyla would find that peace, too. When it came to her, he wanted a lot of things. But this was what he wanted most.

Kyla glanced up at the gate signs, making her way through a throng of people who'd just gotten off a plane from San Diego. She was looking for a flight from Denver, where Stella had her layover on the way to Eugene.

"Excuse me!"

A young woman pushed past, running toward a soldier in fatigues. She jumped into his arms and he spun her around, prompting the crowd around them to burst into applause.

Kyla smiled. But then thought of Ben, whose arms

had only been around her a few precious times, and felt a lump rise in her throat.

It was better this way. It really was. They'd never really had a chance, anyway. No matter how she felt about him, the whole thing was just too complicated. They had too much history stretching between them, and that was the cold hard truth of it.

She looked at her watch. The plane would be landing any minute now. And the thought of getting to hug her foster sister again was almost enough to put the smile back on her face.

Stella had called the night before last, telling her and Frances that she was coming home. It would be a short visit, but long enough to spend some time together, and talk about the future. She said she'd be coming back at the end of the summer to stay. At that, Frances had argued, but in true Stella fashion, she'd just brushed it off. "I'm coming home, Frances," she said haughtily. "Better get used to it." There wasn't much Frances could say to that, since her oldest foster daughter had gotten so much of this stubbornness directly from her.

Kyla came to a stop near the gate from Denver, and watched as the passengers began to walk through the tunnel and rotating glass doors that led to the main terminal. Some of them were being met by family or friends, others looked travel weary, making their way directly to the luggage carousel not far away.

Standing on her tiptoes, she tried to see over their

heads. Trying to see Stella in the crowd. Her heart thumped inside her chest, reminding her how long it had been since they'd seen each other. Frances had pushed back on this visit, but the truth was, she was thrilled. Both her girls under one roof. The only one missing now was Marley.

Kyla grinned as a curvy brunette came into view. Her long hair hung in ripples down her back, her blue eyes twinkling. When she saw Kyla, she smiled wide.

"Oh my God," she said, reaching out and putting her hands on Kyla's shoulders. "Let me look at you. Stunning, as usual."

"Stop it. You're the one who's stunning."

"We must get it from Frances."

Stella winked before pulling her into a hug. She always smelled like flowers, even in the middle of winter. Kyla had given up trying to figure out if it was her shampoo, or a body spray or if she'd just been born smelling like this, but she'd missed it. It brought her right back to childhood.

After a minute, Kyla pulled away. "I can't believe you're actually here."

"In the flesh."

"Marley said you'd probably come, but still…"

"The three of us, or none of us, remember?" She hooked her pinky finger in Kyla's. It had been their secret handshake as kids, something they did every time they saw each other. Kyla remembered it making her feel special—like she was part of something unique, which of course, she was.

"And Marley would be here too," Stella continued, "if it wasn't for that dumb boss of hers."

Kyla laughed. "Yeah, I heard about him."

"She's got to quit. Come work for the Tiger Sharks."

"I don't know that she'd ever come back here for good. Too many bad memories."

"We've all got those. But Frances needs us. And we can make new memories, right?" Stella linked her arm in hers. "Let's go. I carried on, so no suitcases to pick up."

"How long are you staying?"

"Only three days. But we can get a lot figured out by the time I leave. Take some walks on the beach, hunt some agates?"

That sounded good. It was music to Kyla's ears, really. But she'd eventually have to tell Stella about her plan to leave Christmas Bay, which she wasn't looking forward to. It probably wouldn't come as a surprise; nobody had expected her to stay forever. Still, she now had to admit that she'd begun to explore the idea of staying without even realizing it. That's what this last month with Ben had done to her. She'd always loved him. But she'd started *falling* in love with him, which was a feeling that had hit her like a freight train. Now she just had to un-fall in love with him. It was laughable really.

Stella looked over at her as they walked. "What's wrong, Kyla?"

"Nothing. Nothing's wrong."

"Baloney. You're too quiet."

"I am?"

She was stalling now. It was obvious.

"You know you are." Stella squeezed her arm. "This wouldn't be about Ben Martinez, would it?"

"What? I don't..."

Stella smiled. "You forget—I talk to Frances, too."

"Good Lord. What did she tell you?"

"Only that you've been spending some time together. And I know this has to thrill you, because you've had a thing for this guy since grade school. If memory serves."

Kyla shook her head. "No. Nope. I *had* a thing for him in grade school. But then he turned my mom in..."

"And he's still the unlucky sap with the target on his forehead, right?"

Kyla pursed her lips at this, looking straight ahead.

Stella slowed down and turned to her. "Kyla."

"What?"

"Stop for a minute and look at me, will you?"

Stella was only two years older than Kyla, three years older than Marley, but she'd always taken her big sister role seriously. And they'd always listened to her, even when they hadn't wanted to. Even when they'd been trying their best to rebel.

Kyla came to a stop and faced her foster sister with a sigh. "What, Stella?"

"Want to tell me what's really going on here?"

"No."

"Too bad. You know I'll get it out of you eventually."

"A tickle fight in the middle of the airport?"

"Not necessarily. But don't put it past me, either. Now what is it?"

Kyla bit the inside of her cheek. Harder than she'd meant. She'd known Stella would find out about Ben in time, but she hadn't expected to have to tackle the subject so soon. Before they'd even left the airport. If she couldn't even talk about him without difficulty, she was in much deeper than she'd thought.

"Kyla," Stella said softly. People brushed past them, hustling to their gates. Somewhere close a baby cried. But all of a sudden, everything else fell away, and it was just the two of them standing there. Stella had always been able to see into Kyla's heart and read it like a book. It was stupid to think she'd be able to keep any of this from her, even for a day or two.

She took a deep breath. "I went and fell in love with him," she said. "I don't know how it happened. It just did, even though I tried not to. But he's kind of amazing, and he's got this daughter who's amazing, too. And it all just scares the hell out of me."

Stella gave her a small, empathetic smile. "Of course it does, honey. Because you have trust issues up the keister."

"Ha. Say what you really feel."

"You know I love you. You know that, right?"

Kyla nodded.

"So, listen to me when I say that we *all* have trust issues. And at some point we have to face them."

"I'm not ready."

"I'm not saying you should be. But not facing them is starting to impact your life. And I get it. I've kissed a few relationships goodbye that…" She shrugged, suddenly looking sad. "Well, who knows. But the point is, I get it. I'm just asking you to slow down and don't rush through this. Don't run from it. Face it. And then if you decide he's not right for you, you'll know you did it the *right* way."

Kyla let this settle. It was the same thing Frances had told her the other night. It was the same thing she kept telling herself, but the problem was, the instinct to run was so strong, it nearly overwhelmed her every time she thought of Ben. The need to protect herself always won out. Always. The question was, would she ever be able to break the cycle? The only way to do that was to make herself vulnerable again. She had to trust that Ben wouldn't hurt her, and if he did, she'd just have to heal and move on like a normal person.

But she wasn't a normal person. She was Kyla Beckett, who had trust issues up the keister.

She smiled and shook her head.

"What?" Stella asked.

"Just thinking. We're all so screwed up."

"Bet your ass. But that's what gives us character, right?"

Kyla laughed. "Are you hungry? We can grab some Thai before we head back."

"Sounds good—I'm starving."

They began walking again, headed toward the airport's front entrance.

"Frances told me about this kid she hired," Stella said. "Hunter? Tell me what happened with that."

Kyla took a deep breath. He hadn't been back into Coastal Sweets since she'd made the phone call to CPS last week. Her heart hurt so much for him that sometimes she'd tear up when she thought about it. Hunter's road wasn't going to be easy. In fact, she knew exactly how hard it would be.

She began telling Stella the story from the very beginning. From that fateful morning when he'd stolen their tip jar, and had set everything in motion.

For better or worse.

"Frances, what are you feeding him?" Stella stared down at Jacques who was stretched out in a sunbeam under the window. He looked like he was about to have kittens. It was a fair question.

"Just cat food," Frances said innocently. "The wet kind."

"And how many cans of that a day?"

Kyla grinned at that and looked over at Frances who wouldn't look at either one of them. Whether or not she overfed Jacques was an ongoing debate between her and Stella. Unfortunately, the proof was in the cat food.

"Okay," Stella said. "I'll take that as, no less than three cans a day."

"*Two* cans," Frances insisted. "With some snacks on the side."

There was no point arguing. Kyla knew Jacques might have to explode before Frances would ever admit she had a problem.

Her foster mother leaned back in her chair, and took a sip of her iced tea. "I'm so glad you're home, honey," she said to Stella. "Even though you'd like to put Jacques on a diet."

"I love him fat. It's just not good for him. And I'm glad I'm home, too."

"And you're leaving when?"

Stella glanced over at Kyla, a worried look on her face. She'd just told Frances when she was leaving. By now Kyla was used to this kind of memory lapse, but it was obviously unsettling for Stella.

"Uh… Tuesday," she answered quietly. "I'm leaving Tuesday."

Frances frowned, reading her expression. "Did you already tell me that?"

"I did, but it's okay."

"It's really not." Frances looked out the window, a deep wrinkle between her brows.

"No," Stella said. "You're right. It's not. And it's not fair, either. But we're going to roll with it, just like you taught us. Together."

Frances glanced back at her and smiled. "I did teach you that."

"You taught us a lot of things. Most of all, you taught us how to be a family. And I know Kyla has said this too, but you're not going to have to do this alone."

"I know. You're such good girls."

"I think you should consider going back to the doctor," Kyla said. "Just for a checkup."

Frances gave her a sharp look.

"I'm not talking about a diagnosis," she said quickly. "But I do think we should do our best to get educated, so we know *how* to roll with it."

It had been something she'd wanted to say for a while now, but Frances had been so adamant about the no doctor thing that Kyla knew she wouldn't have heard it. But somehow, with Stella here, there seemed to be a subtle shift in her thinking. It was like she was more willing to listen. More willing to accept. And that was a relief.

"Kyla's right," Stella said. "That's the smart thing to do."

"And it just so happens that we know a fantastic nurse-practitioner," Kyla said.

Frances nodded slowly. "True. And going to Isabel would be more like visiting a friend."

"A friend who's been to medical school," Stella said.

"I guess you're right," Frances said. "It's probably a good idea."

Stella leaned forward in her chair. "We also need to talk about something else, Frances," she said quietly.

Putting her teacup down, Frances raised her chin. "I already know what you're going to say, but go ahead."

Stella glanced over at Kyla again. They'd talked about this on the way over. It was time to bring up what to do with the house and the candy shop. Not right away, but eventually. Eventually they'd need a solid plan to fall back on. And like trying to convince Frances to go to the doctor, they knew it would be an uphill battle.

Kyla tried her best to ignore the nerves in her belly, and leaned forward in her chair, too. "This house is so much work for you, Frances," she said. "And we worry about you up here all alone. We've talked about it, and decided that at least one of us will be in Christmas Bay from here on out—"

Frances held up a hand, cutting her off. "How in the world are you going to do that?"

"I'm going to come home," Stella said.

"No. I can't let you do that."

"Frances, I can work anywhere. I'm a free spirit, remember? I love the shop—you know that. I can help you there for a while and see how it goes."

"And I won't be far away, either," Kyla said. "I know several schools that are hiring close by."

She also knew of a position at Christmas Bay Middle School that, incidentally, she'd be perfect for. Seventh grade social studies. She'd seen it online a few weeks ago, but hadn't let herself think any more about it. She was leaving. Still, though, it had popped into her head just now, and her heart skipped before she could put it in its place.

Frances looked like she wanted to argue. But she also looked relieved. There was no doubt. "I don't know what to say…"

"We can figure things out as we go," Kyla said. "But the house, Frances. We need to talk about the house."

At that, Frances clasped her hands stiffly in her lap. This was probably what she'd been expecting.

"I know how you feel about this place," Stella said. "We love it, too. It's home. But it's so big. It's so much for you to take care of."

"I'm not moving," Frances said. "No."

"We're not asking you to," Kyla said softly. "All we're asking is for you to be open to it when the time comes."

"And moving out eventually doesn't mean giving it up altogether," Stella said. "You could keep it, turn it into an Airbnb when you're ready."

"A *family* needs to live here, Stella," Frances said emphatically. "A family has always lived here."

Kyla studied her. It was true. Frances's grandparents had raised her mother here. Her mother had raised her here. And Frances had raised her foster daughters here, as well. It wasn't just a house. It was part of her heart and soul, and the thought of leaving it was clearly too much to bear.

"You're absolutely right," Stella said. "I'm sorry."

"You don't have to be sorry, honey. It makes

sense. I'm stubborn, but I'm not unreasonable. I'm just not ready yet. I only want this place to be loved the way I love it. That's all."

It was the first time Kyla had heard her accept, even partially, the idea of leaving the house. And hopefully she wouldn't have to go anywhere for a long time. But it was important progress, and it made her feel better.

Stella seemed to feel better, too. She exhaled softly, and leaned down to pick Jacques up off the floor. The cat immediately began purring as she held his squishy body close to her chest.

"I've missed this," she said into his fur. "There's no place like home, right?"

Kyla smiled.

No, there really wasn't.

Chapter Fourteen

Ben made his way through the farmers' market, aware of the looks he was getting in his uniform. Most people nodded politely and said hello, knowing him by name. Others weren't so friendly. This was the portion of the population he'd had to arrest on drunken Friday nights, or pull over for going fifty in a twenty-five. He was used to it. All part of being a police officer in a small town. You weren't going to avoid the folks who didn't like you.

He glanced around at the stands, their Fourth of July streamers billowing in the breeze. He hadn't seen Gabe Mohatt for a few weeks now, and he couldn't decide if that was good or bad. Maybe he simply left town after the CPS investigation, sick of the law in general. God knows his family would be better off.

Ben still had an unsettling feeling about it, though. Gabe wasn't the type to go down without a fight. Then again, Ben always expected trouble, whether it was likely to happen or not.

He walked slowly through the crowd, keeping an eye out for shoplifters or arguments among the vendors, which weren't uncommon. It was a nice Saturday afternoon—warm for the coast, which also meant the market was packed today, with a lot of people looped from the beer tent a few yards away. Tomorrow was the Fourth, and the atmosphere was already buzzing.

As for how he and Gracie would be spending the holiday, they were going to have Isabel, Jason and the boys over to barbecue hot dogs, and do sparklers in the backyard. A far cry from his bachelor days, when he would've closed that beer tent down himself.

Rubbing the back of his neck, he stopped in front of a flower stand and looked down at the bouquets. Daisies, lilies…lots of other things that he couldn't name, but that reminded him of his mom's garden growing up. He'd picked flowers for his prom date from that garden. He'd gone with a snobby girl named Rebecca who hadn't wanted to take a picture because her hair hadn't looked right. He couldn't even remember why he'd asked her now. In fact, he couldn't even remember what had drawn him to Sam in the first place. They'd never been right for each other. Never.

He stared down at the flowers, and for the first

time, maybe ever, there was a feeling of relief deep inside. Not at her leaving, exactly. And sure as hell not at her leaving Gracie. But maybe it was knowing that if she hadn't done something, he never would have. He would've stayed with her forever, because he didn't quit on his family.

So, she'd freed him. The question now was, what was he going to do with that freedom? What was he going to do with his future?

Ben looked up when a young woman approached from behind the table. She was pretty—red hair pulled into a ponytail, a green apron tied snug around her waist. She smiled up at him, and he recognized that smile. There was some insinuation there. Probably the uniform. He'd found that old theory to be absolutely true, which, for his single officers, was a definite perk of the job.

"Bellis perennis," she said, her pink lips glistening.

"I'm sorry?"

"It's the scientific name. But it sounds much more impressive than what they're actually called, which is the common daisy."

He looked back down at the flowers. "Oh."

"Are you shopping for someone special?" she asked. "We can make you a bouquet if you don't see anything you like."

He'd had his hands splayed out on the table, and her gaze flickered to his left one. She was wondering if he was married. *Definitely the uniform.*

He took a step back and put them in his pockets. "No," he said. "Just looking. They're very pretty."

"Thank you. We'll be here next week, too. Every Sunday through the summer. If you ever decided to come back for anything…"

He nodded. "I'll keep that in mind. Have a good Fourth."

"You too, Officer."

After one more lingering look, she finally turned to help another customer, this one with her wallet out, asking about tea roses. And he and his uniform were forgotten, swallowed up by everyday life, and the hustle of trying to make a buck.

"Ben!"

He glanced over at someone waving through the smoke coming from the barbecue tent. He didn't know what they had on the grill, but it smelled amazing.

He waved back, unable to tell who it was. There were too many people in line for barbecue, and they were standing right behind a guy in a cowboy hat.

He turned to go.

"Wait!"

Again, he looked over. And this time recognized Kyla making her way through the crowd. She was with another woman, curvy, long dark hair, but he only had eyes for Kyla, who, for the first time in two weeks, looked like she might be happy to see him.

She smiled as they approached, and the effect that had on him was immediate. The attraction to her, the overwhelming desire to touch her again, was all-consuming. And he had to school his features to make sure he didn't make an ass out of himself right there in public.

"I was worried you weren't going to stop," she said. "You looked like you were in another world."

He swallowed, his tongue feeling thick and dry in his mouth. Of course he couldn't tell her that he'd been thinking about his future, about how to move on from Sam once and for all. And that it all circled back to Kyla in the end.

He couldn't say that, so he just turned to the woman she was with, and held out his hand for something productive to do.

"Ben Martinez," he said.

She smiled wide. "Stella Clarke. I used to live here, but you probably don't remember me. I was younger than you."

"You're…"

"Kyla's foster sister. Frances raised me, too."

A slow realization crept over him. He'd heard all about Stella and Marley from Frances, but he'd never met them before. He knew the three girls had grown up close, and were still close.

"It's nice to meet you," he said.

"It's nice to meet you, too. I've heard a ton about you from Kyla here."

Kyla shot her a look. So, she'd been talking about him. Interesting.

Watching her, he put his hands back in his pockets. She looked beautiful today, but she looked beautiful every day. Her dark hair was loose and wavy, and she wore a pair of faded denim overalls over a white tank top. She'd gotten some sun recently; he could tell. Freckles were scattered over her nose, and her shoulders were a little pink. She was lovely.

"How are you doing?" he asked, hoping his voice didn't sound strained.

She gazed back, and there was something in her expression that made his heart ache. She seemed vulnerable right then, with the people brushing past, and the live band starting to play across the grassy area—something country and vaguely sad.

"Hunter hasn't been back," she said.

He frowned. He wasn't surprised, but he'd still been hoping it would work out somehow. That Hunter would want to come back to the shop, or be allowed to come back by his parents. But life didn't always end up like you hoped. He knew that better than most. And so did Kyla.

"I'm sorry," he said. "I really am."

"There's nothing to be sorry for. We did the best we could for him. You were right. You were right about a lot of things. It just took me a while to get there."

He gazed at her steadily, unable to take his eyes off her. Realizing that she looked very different today. There was a distinctive peace that had settled over her features since he'd seen her last.

"And honestly?" she said. "I've been missing you."

He didn't trust himself to speak right then, so he stayed quiet. People kept walking past, but he barely noticed.

"I'm not sure what to do with that," she continued quietly, "because I've decided you and I are the worst idea ever."

But she said it with a tilt to her lips, a certain warmth in her eyes that was hard to ignore.

"Oh, yeah?" he said.

"And, you know. I'm moving away from here. So I won't have to see you."

"And when will that be?"

"As soon as possible."

"Good," he said. "Because I'm sick of seeing you, too."

Smiling, she looked down at that.

"Uh, I hate to interrupt this charming exchange with the overtly sexual undertones," Stella said with a smirk, "but Frances is waiting for her barbecue."

Kyla's cheeks colored. There was no mistaking it. They flushed a lovely pink, making those new freckles almost disappear.

"Are you going to be around after the holiday?" she asked him. "I have some gummy worms set aside for Gracie that I've been meaning to drop by the station."

"I'll be there," he said.

"It was nice to meet you, Ben," Stella said.

"You, too."

She tugged on Kyla's arm. "Come on, lover girl."

This time Kyla laughed, and let herself be led away.

But not before turning to look at him one more time.

"That'll be eight fifty," Kyla said, bagging up some caramels for the lady in a Christmas Bay sweatshirt that still had the tag attached. It was poking out the back of the neckhole—a cheerful announcement that this was most definitely a tourist.

"This place is so cute," the woman said, handing over a ten.

Kyla didn't know if she was talking about the town or the shop, but it didn't really matter. It all went hand in hand.

"I told my husband I want to retire here," she continued.

"Oh? Where are you from?"

"Arizona. Phoenix."

"But it's so nice there. So much sun."

"It is nice, but there are a lot of people. I'm sick of people."

Kyla laughed, handing back her change. "I hear that."

"And this little town…" The woman paused, shaking her head. The tag bobbed behind her ear. "There's something about it. It has a pull to it, you know? Something different."

Kyla did know. She knew very well. That pull, that something different, was what had brought her back after all these years. It was keeping her here now. Of course, Frances had been the main reason at first. But now there were more reasons popping up like flowers in a garden. Ben was one, her first love. Who'd later become her greatest adversary, and then, inexplicably, her love again. Gracie was another—the adorable little girl who had shown Kyla that just because you'd been hurt before, didn't mean you couldn't love again. It didn't mean you couldn't trust again. You just had to open your heart to do it.

So, yes. She understood that pull.

"You live here?" the woman asked, tucking a few dollars into the tip jar.

A simple question, but one that made Kyla's heart skip a beat just the same. Did she live here? When she'd come back at the beginning of the summer, the answer to that would've been a hard no. Now she wasn't so sure. Because the thought of it made her heart do things like skip a beat. That wasn't something she could ignore any longer. It just wasn't.

"I used to," she said quietly. "I might again. This is where my family is."

"Oh, then you definitely should. Family is everything."

Kyla nodded. It absolutely was.

"Well, I sure enjoyed your little shop. I'll try and come back before we leave on Friday."

"I hope you do. And if you retire here, don't be a stranger."

The woman smiled. "I won't."

Kyla watched her walk out the door, feeling happier than she had in weeks. She knew Stella's visit had something to do with that. They'd talked with Frances, and at least had a short-term plan laid out.

But there was something else responsible for it, too. She was in love with Ben. She now knew that was a fact. An inexplicable fact? Maybe. But she was starting to wonder if it was more like destiny. Like she'd been meant to come back here to fall in love with him. It was a romantic thought that was beginning to nestle its way inside her heart.

The bell above the door tinkled, and she looked up, tugged away from her thoughts.

And there, standing with his hands in his jean pockets, and looking somehow much older, was Hunter.

Her stomach dropped. *Hunter.* She'd been waiting for him to come back this whole time. To swear at her, to blame her for what she'd done. To twist her emotions into a complicated mess that she knew she might never untangle completely. She'd been waiting for him, and had started to think he'd probably never come.

Yet, here he was. Wearing a shy smile. Not looking at all like he blamed her for anything.

Her chest warmed.

"You're back," she said. It was all she could manage. She was afraid she was going to start crying, and that would just be embarrassing for them both.

He nodded. He'd gotten a haircut. She could see his bright blue eyes clearly now, how they twinkled in the morning light.

"I wanted to say goodbye," he said.

"Goodbye?"

She walked out from behind the counter. It wasn't just her imagination. He did look older. More mature, but lighter in a way. It suited him.

"My mom and I are moving," he said. "My aunt lives in Eugene, and has a job lined up for her. She and my uncle have been trying to get us to come for a long time. They're pretty happy about it."

"And are you happy about it?" she asked.

"I can finally have a dog. And my mom is excited about her job. I've never really seen her like this before. It's nice."

She watched him steadily.

"She decided to leave my dad," he said. "After... well. You know."

Taking a step toward him, she clasped her hands in front of her belly. "Hunter, I'm so sorry."

"They never said it was you and Frances, but I knew. I mean, you were the only people I've talked to about my dad."

Her eyes stung with tears and she blinked them back. This scene was so familiar, that all of a sudden, she found herself tumbling back, back. To where she could see her mother now—curled in a ball on the couch, so out of it that Kyla thought she was about to die. And then she did die.

Kyla used to blame Ben for that. And then herself. And her mother, too. But now, as she looked at Hunter, and saw how clearly his luck was about to change, she knew she was done with blame. She only wanted to forgive.

"We just wanted to keep you safe," she said. "I know how hard it is when you love someone, but they're hurting you. Sometimes it doesn't have to be physical. Sometimes there are other types of pain that are just as hard to take. And I'm just so sorry you had to go through that."

Hunter looked down at his sneakers. One of the laces was untied, and dragged the floor like a worm. Like a gummy worm...

If she never saw him again, she knew she'd always remember him like this. Somewhere between a boy and a man. About to embark on a new life. Hopefully a *better* life. Not unlike the one she'd found once, with her foster family in the big house on the cape.

"Thank you for caring enough to do something," Hunter said. "It feels good. To have friends like this."

"We'll always be your friends. We'll always be right here if you need us."

The bell tinkled above the door, and a group of chattering kids walked in.

"Well," Hunter said. "I'd better get going."

"Wait." Kyla picked up the tip jar and handed it

over. It was full this morning. Frances had forgotten to empty it again last night.

A slow smile spread across his face. "But why?"

"For a housewarming present," she said. "And because you deserve it."

He looked at her for a few seconds, then stepped forward to give her a quick hug. It was awkward, sweet, heartbreaking and wonderful.

"My mom doesn't like to say goodbye," he said, pulling away again. "She says, see you later."

"Well, then. See you later, kid."

He grinned. "Later."

And then he was gone. Tip jar and all.

Ben sat at his desk, the sun slanting golden and warm through the blinds. The day was finally winding down, and he was glad. It had been a long week, and he was looking forward to going home to a cold beer and a baseball game on TV.

Closing the file he'd been reading through, he leaned back and rubbed his eyes. Gracie was at Isabel's tonight, so he was on his own. He guessed most parents in his position might be happy for the break. But he missed that little munchkin when she was gone.

"Chief?"

He looked up to see his receptionist in the doorway.

"Getting ready to close up, Ellen?"

"I just have one more report to enter, then I'm

done. But there's someone up front to see you." She frowned. "She says she has a worm delivery?"

He laughed. "You can send her back."

After a few seconds, Kyla appeared in his doorway holding the distinctive white bag that always made Gracie lose her damn mind.

Her gray gaze settled on him, warming his very bones.

"I'm glad I caught you," she said. "I had to run to get here before five."

"With gummy worms."

She shook the bag. "We have to keep our fans happy, you know."

"They're a nice bonus, but she'd be a fan of yours, with or without the worms."

"Now, that's not a sentence you hear every day."

"Please," he said, motioning toward the chair opposite his desk. "Sit."

"I'm not holding you up?"

"No. I'm glad to see you."

She pulled out the chair and sank into it with a smile. "You said you were tired of seeing me the other day."

"I say a lot of things. Mostly to throw you off."

"Oh yeah?"

He studied her, feeling some of the hesitation from the last month start to ease away. Feeling himself relax into this new feeling, and not wanting to question it. What he wanted more than anything was to trust it, and to let it carry him where it was going naturally.

And where would that be? There was only one way to find out.

He leaned back in his chair and laced his hands behind his head. "What would you say if I asked you out?"

She stared at him. "Asked me out…"

"On a date. Not a playdate. A date, date."

One corner of her mouth tilted, and he imagined kissing it, and then moving his way down the graceful column of her neck.

"What about all the reasons not to?" she asked.

"What about them?"

"You said it wasn't a good idea."

"I say a lot of things, remember? I changed my mind."

She put the bag on the desk and pushed it toward him. A peace offering, maybe? He could do a lot worse.

"I've been thinking a lot over the last few weeks," she said quietly. "About everything."

He'd been thinking, too. The question was, had they come to the same place? Could they meet somewhere in the middle like two people who were learning to live again? It was hard not to hold his breath for the answer.

He regarded her, that gaze of hers so familiar that it broke his heart. All of a sudden, he saw her as a little girl again—in baggy jeans and smudged glasses.

And he wanted to pull her close, and tell her it was all going to be okay. That he would keep her safe. Safe in his arms for as long as she'd allow it.

"Hunter came into the shop today," she said. "He came to say goodbye."

He leaned forward and put his elbows on his desk. It was so quiet, he could hear the clock ticking in the hallway.

"Goodbye," he said. "Where's he going?"

"He and his mom and are moving to Eugene to be with his aunt and uncle. She's got a job lined up there."

He nodded. So, she was leaving the asshole. Good for her. And she had a support system, which meant it might actually take. God, he hoped so. He hoped they'd leave here and find exactly what they were looking for.

"He seemed happy," Kyla said. "And it all started to come full circle for me. His situation, my childhood. You gave me the chance at a future that Hunter is getting now. You did that for me."

His throat tightened. "I didn't do that for you, Kyla. You did that for yourself."

Silence settled between them. There was the faint jingle of Ellen's keys as she locked up for the day. Outside, the sun sank lower, its color turning a deeper, more meaningful hue. His office was bathed in gold.

"I'm sorry I've been blaming you," Kyla said. "I needed someone other than my mom to blame, because admitting that she failed me felt like admitting she didn't love me. I know she loved me. But she was sick. She made mistakes. And she paid for them."

Kyla had grown into such a strong woman; he doubted she even knew how strong. But there would always be a softness there, deep down. A tenderness that made her special.

"I forgive her," she said, her voice trembling a little. "I'm choosing to forgive her."

Without a word, he pushed away from his desk and came around to where she was sitting. He held out his hand, and she took it.

He helped her to her feet and she stood there looking up at him with that tenderness in her eyes. He knew it was for him. It was also for her mother, and Frances, and Hunter. And everyone else who'd come into her life and changed it in one way or another.

He brushed his fingertips underneath her chin. "What do you say to that date?" he asked. "We can have some coffee. Maybe get to know each other again."

"Actually," she said, "that sounds perfect."

Chapter Fifteen

"Are you sure you don't want to come?" Frances asked, putting on her sweater.

Outside, the streetlamps were just coming on, illuminating the wet sidewalk in silver. The rain had stopped, and the clouds had cleared in the night sky overhead. Stars twinkled there like fireflies.

Frances was already late. Bingo at the community center started at eight sharp. But they'd had inventory that day, and she was a stickler when it came to inventory. Now that they were finished, though, it looked like she'd have time for a few games. And maybe even some leftover popcorn if she hurried.

"I don't think so," Kyla said. "I'm beat. But I'd love to drive you…"

Frances shot her a look. "I promised to let you

girls start helping me more. But I can get to bingo just fine. It's only a block away, straight as an arrow. And Donna is going to meet me at the door, so you don't have to worry."

Kyla smiled. She was trying not to; she really was. "Okay. But you've got your phone in case you need me?"

"I've got my phone, but I won't need you. Donna is giving me a ride home and I'll be fine." Frances gave her a quick peck on the cheek. "I promise, honey. And don't forget Jacques."

"I won't." Actually, she might've if Frances hadn't said anything. The cat had taken to sleeping in the storage room lately, his princess bed abandoned on the counter. He'd found some leftover Bubble Wrap that made for a cushier experience apparently, and Jacques and cushy went hand in paw.

"Don't wait up!" Frances waved and was out the door before Kyla could tell her to be careful.

She watched out the window as her foster mother headed down the sidewalk and toward the community center in the distance. Only a block. She'd be fine.

Still, Kyla had a funny feeling that she couldn't seem to shake. She'd had it all day. At first, she thought it was because she hadn't heard from Ben. He'd taken Gracie deep sea fishing on his friend's boat earlier, but he'd texted a few hours ago. They were home safely, and he was getting ready to work the graveyard shift because one of his officers had called in sick.

So, that wasn't it. Kyla had never believed in premonitions, but as she stood there with her stomach in a strange knot, she told herself she might have to drive by the community center on her way home. Just in case.

She stretched her arms over her head and yawned. She hadn't been lying when she said she was beat. Her back ached from bending over their inventory all afternoon, and suddenly all she wanted was to get home and run a hot bath. Maybe she'd make some tea afterward, and see if that position at the middle school was still open. She hoped with a sudden pang that it still was.

Smiling to herself, she turned toward the darkened storeroom. "Jacques, here, kitty kitty! Let's go home."

She waited, looking at the spot underneath the lowest shelf where he liked to stuff himself, but he didn't appear.

"Jacques. Come on—let's go."

She really didn't want to have to bend down and pull him out. Her muscles were screaming.

"Jacques—"

He meowed behind her. She turned to see him sitting near the front window, his tail twitching back and forth. He was staring out into the darkness, ignoring her completely.

"What are you doing, you crazy cat?" She could hear the slight edge to her voice. Ever since the incident with the guy in black a few weeks ago, she'd made sure not to linger too long after closing. It had unsettled her enough that it was the first thing that popped into her head now. Especially since she'd forgotten to lock the door behind Frances when she'd left.

She reached for her purse and dug around for the keys. *Stupid.* She needed to be more careful.

Jacques meowed again, and she twisted around to look. She couldn't see anything through the darkened window, but this was so unlike him that chills marched up the back of her neck. She had to remind herself that she didn't believe in premonitions. Or overweight cats suddenly warning of impending danger. It was probably just a squirrel or something. At night. In the middle of town…

She turned her attention back to her purse and dug around some more. Where the hell were they? This was ridiculous.

With trembling hands, she plopped it down on the counter. She pulled her cell phone out. Her wallet, her makeup bag, her sunglasses. And there, in the very corner, were the keys.

She sighed. *Good Lord.* At this rate, she was going to have to start wearing them around her neck.

She plucked them out and turned toward the front door again, but jumped when she saw a man standing on the other side of the glass.

"What the *hell*?"

He stood in a shadow underneath the awning, looking unsettlingly familiar in his dark clothes.

Her thoughts bounced around chaotically, trying to find purchase. It was probably the same guy from a few weeks ago. It'd be too much of a coincidence otherwise. Which meant he wanted something, or was trying to scare her. And since he'd decided to show up after closing both times, the second scenario seemed most likely.

"What do you want?" she asked, loud enough that he'd be able to hear through the glass. She really needed to go lock the door in his face, but was having trouble taking the first step toward him. All her instincts screamed to stay as far away as possible.

Swaying a little, he reached for the door handle.

Jacques hissed and pinned his ears back. Then darted into the storage room, knocking the broom over as he skittered past. Kyla gaped after him, unable to believe what she'd just seen.

The door opened with a soft *swoosh*, and she looked quickly back at it, the cat forgotten. The man stepped inside, and she took a step backward toward her phone.

"We're closed," she managed.

It was an absurd thing to say; of course they were closed. And it was obvious this guy wasn't here for candy. But her brain didn't seem to want to come to the conclusion that he might be here for something else.

She watched him, knowing he was drunk. She

could smell his sour breath from where she stood. His eyes were maybe the palest shade of blue she'd ever seen. Something about him looked familiar, but again, her brain wasn't connecting the dots. It was like she was moving underwater. This was something that happened in the movies, not in a candy shop in Christmas Bay.

"I know you're closed, you dumb bitch," he slurred.

She reached for her phone on the counter, but was shaking so hard, she ended up batting it further away.

"You need to leave," she said, her voice sounding miraculously firm. She actually felt like she was having a heart attack. "Or I'm going to call the police."

His mouth stretched into a grin. "Oh, you're going to call the police? Like you called the county about my boy?"

Kyla's stomach dropped. *Oh, no. Oh, God.* No wonder he looked familiar. This was Hunter's dad.

All of a sudden, the pieces shifted and fell into place. His wife had finally left him. She'd moved with their son to another city. He was drunk and alone and pissed off. And he blamed her for all of it.

Without taking her eyes off him, she reached for the phone again, this time grabbing on to it with a vise grip.

She stepped quickly behind the counter and dialed 911.

"You think you can just screw with people's lives like this?" he said, ignoring the fact that she was obviously calling the police. It was like he didn't care.

About anything. The look on his face said it all. He had nothing left to lose.

Kyla kept an eye on him closely as the phone rang once. And then a dispatcher picked up.

"911, what's your emergency?"

"I'm calling from Coastal Sweets on Main," she said. "We have an intruder. Please hurry."

"Ma'am, I have a unit—"

With catlike quickness, he reached out and slapped the phone out of her hand. It went flying and hit the wall behind her.

She gasped. Her ear rang, the side of her face going numb.

"You thought I wouldn't *come* for you?" he said. "Is that what you thought?"

Kyla twisted around, looking for the phone.

"You're not calling anybody," he said quietly. "I never touched my kid."

She turned on him then, triggered by the words. *Liar.* He was a liar and a coward. Unable to take any kind of responsibility. Unable to admit that he was a lousy father. Unable, or unwilling to try and do better. She thought of her mother then, and how their life together had been destroyed because of those very same traits.

Fury rose in her chest like fire, sparking and cracking, and giving her courage where there hadn't been much before. Maybe this was the gift that her mom had finally bestowed on her all these years later.

Maybe she was reaching across time and space, and saying, see? Something good came of it after all...

"Don't you stand there and lie to me," Kyla hissed. "I know better. You should be ashamed of yourself."

"And you should learn your place."

He lunged forward and grabbed her before she could bolt. He squeezed her arm viciously and twisted it around. This close, he smelled even worse, and her eyes began to water. She was terrified of what he might do. But she was also livid that he had the nerve to come in here like this. To put his hands on her. To put his hands on his own son.

"Let me go!" she screamed, kicking him square between the legs.

He doubled over with a grunt, but held tight.

From across the shop, someone hit the door with such force that it shattered. In the furthest corner of her mind, she was aware of the glass tinkling to the floor.

And then that someone was pulling Gabe Mohatt off her with a deep, guttural sound that she knew she'd remember forever. A man, also in black. Tall and broad chested, with a silver badge pinned to it.

Ben. Her Ben...

"Get on the floor!" he growled. *"Now!"*

She blinked, her eyes filling with tears. They spilled down her cheeks as she stumbled backward and leaned against the wall for support. She watched the two men struggle a few feet away, but truthfully, it wasn't much of a struggle. Ben had Gabe pinned to the floor, his knee planted firmly in his back. And then the handcuffs were on.

"Forty-seven twenty-one," Ben panted into the mic on his shoulder.

The radio crackled. "Go ahead."

"Code four, one in custody. Send backup code three, please."

"Copy that."

Kyla stood there staring down at him, holding her arm which was now starting to throb. *Ben.* In his crisp uniform, with his dark eyes flashing.

After a minute, they found hers, and his gaze immediately softened. "Are you okay, Kyla?"

She nodded, unable to speak.

A moment later, there were red-and-blue lights flashing outside. And more police officers walking through the shattered door, their boots crunching on the glass.

One of them hauled Gabe Mohatt to his feet and began reading him his rights. And then Ben was there. Pulling her into his arms, saying gentle things in her ear that she was having trouble understanding.

She just clung to him. As if her life depended on it. Because a few minutes ago, it actually had.

"You're safe," she realized he was saying over and over again. "You're safe now."

Kyla sat curled up on the couch the next afternoon, watching the fire crackle in the hearth. Outside, it was chilly, and a light rain pattered against the windows, making the old house feel even cozier.

She could hear Frances puttering around in the kitchen. Her foster mother was in full spoil mode. She'd brought in a plate of cookies earlier—peanut butter, Kyla's favorite. And was now working on sandwiches for lunch.

You have to stop, Kyla had teased her. *Or I'm going to end up weighing as much as Jacques.* Frances had shushed her, of course. And pulled her blanket up farther over her shoulders.

Kyla looked down at the cat now, who was sleeping in a plump black-and-white ball in her lap. She hadn't told anyone what he'd done before Gabe had come into the shop—about the hissing that had been a sign that something was definitely off. Partly because she was afraid they wouldn't believe her. Even Frances, who had a tendency to think Jacques walked on water, might have a hard time with it, since cats weren't exactly like dogs when it came to protecting their people. But mostly, Kyla had kept it to herself because it felt too special to share. An instant that might well have been meant to warn her. Maybe with help from someone from above.

At the moment, she didn't want to think too much about it. She just wanted to sit with Jacques on her lap, listen to him purr and feel grateful that it all turned out okay. She had no doubt that if Ben hadn't come when he had, she might've been struggling for her life. She'd never seen such cold, empty eyes as

Gabe Mohatt's. She knew he was capable of much, much worse than what he'd actually done.

She rubbed her upper arm where a series of black-and-purple bruises had bloomed this morning. He'd yanked it so hard, the EMT who'd looked her over last night thought she might have a rotator cuff injury, and told her to see her doctor to have it checked out. Kyla didn't have a doctor in Christmas Bay, but she had Isabel, who was even better.

Leaning her head back against the couch, she breathed deeply. The woodsmoke from the fire filled her senses, along with the warm, sweet smell of the cookies on the plate next to her. A combination that reminded her of home. Of family. Of love and security that she'd come to know in this house. She was finally beginning to see that, as a person, as a woman, she was healing here. She was getting better.

Frances had so much to do with that. And so did Ben.

He was a concept that had taken a while to accept because she'd been fighting him so hard. At the beginning, she thought she'd have to lose her strength and independence if she allowed herself to need him. Now she knew that allowing herself to need him, or anyone else, was just another stage of her evolution. It wasn't a sign of weakness to need love. It was a sign of strength to welcome it into your life, even after you'd been hurt by it in the past.

So, she guessed she had her mother to thank, too. She'd let Kyla down in so many ways. But she'd also taught her some invaluable lessons, lessons that she was still learning to this day. And in that way, her mom would always be with her—teaching her, and loving her in death, in a way that she hadn't been able to in life.

Kyla stared into the fire, letting her thoughts ebb and flow like tributaries that led to the ocean. Cutting their own path, and showing her the way.

Frances walked in, and patted her knee. Then sat down beside her with a sigh.

"Lunch will be ready in a few," she said. "I'm making some homemade tomato basil soup, your favorite."

"Frances, what would I do without you?"

"Good thing you won't have to find out, honey. You're stuck with me."

"I think we're stuck with each other."

Frances looked toward the fire too, and they gazed at it together, a comforting silence settling between them. It snapped and popped, the sap in the wood hissing every now and then. And then the logs would shift, and the embers would brighten momentarily, glowing orange, like tiny slivers of the sun.

"Did I ever tell you that I was afraid to become a foster parent?" Frances asked quietly.

Gazing at her, Kyla pushed herself up on the couch. "No, I've never heard you say that."

"I was. I was scared to do it. Scared to get attached to children who weren't mine."

Kyla had never heard her say it, but she wasn't

surprised. There were times when she wondered how Frances had done it. She knew there had been other kids, before her and her foster sisters. Kids who had come and gone, who Frances never talked about much. And Kyla had never pushed, because she'd always gotten the feeling that the subject was a tender one.

"What made you change your mind?" she asked.

Frances looked over at her and smiled, the warmth of the fire flushing her cheeks. "Bud."

Her late husband had been the love of her life. When he'd passed away, it had nearly broken Frances in two. They'd had a happy marriage inside this house above Cape Longing, but it hadn't been nearly long enough. And when he'd left her, she'd told Kyla once that she was so lonely it felt like she'd never be happy again.

That was about all Kyla knew of Bud, except for the pictures around the house. He'd had a wonderful, vibrant smile, and kind blue eyes. He looked exactly like a man Frances would love.

"We'd never been able to have kids of our own," Frances said wistfully. "And I wanted to adopt. But Bud wanted to give a home to as many children as possible, for however long they needed one. He had the biggest heart—he was such a good person. He would've been a good dad to you."

Kyla felt a lump rise in her throat. How she would've loved that.

"I never talked about him much when you girls

were growing up," Frances continued, "because it was so painful. But that wasn't the right thing to do. I should have talked about him every day. I should have made sure you all knew him, because he was the reason you came here. He wasn't scared to get attached to any of our kids, because he knew that saying goodbye to them didn't mean we had to stop loving them."

Before Kyla realized that her eyes had filled with tears, they were already spilling down her cheeks.

"Aww, honey," Frances said. "I hope I'm not making you sad by telling you this."

"I'm glad you're telling me. I'm so proud to have grown up in this house, Frances. I hope you know how proud I am, and how much I love you. And how thankful I am that you gave me a home when I needed one the most."

Frances leaned forward. "And I'm just as proud of you. What happened with Hunter…what happened with his dad last night. You were so brave. You welcomed that boy into the shop and into our lives, when I know you had reservations about it. But your heart is big too, Kyla Bear. And now that boy has a fighting chance. He's gone, but you can still love him."

Kyla wiped the tears from her chin. She thought of her mother then. All the good and wonderful things, like her birthday cakes, and her hugs. And she felt an absolute peace spread over her like a warm blanket.

You're gone, but I still love you…

Frances stood, her knees popping, and held out a hand.

"Come on," she said. "The soup is ready."

Ben stood on the doorstep, holding the get-well flowers in one hand, and Gracie's hand in the other. She'd helped pick the bouquet out. Daisies—or as he now knew they were called, common daisies. He was also clutching a bag of gummy worms which Gracie had insisted on.

They'd had to go to the grocery store to get them, as Coastal Sweets was closed for the next few days to have the front door replaced. But he didn't think Kyla would mind.

"Do you think Jacques is making her feel better?" Gracie asked, looking up at him with wide, serious eyes. "He's such a good little fella."

He smiled. "I think Jacques is definitely on duty."

"Do you think he misses his bed at the shop?"

"I bet they brought it home while the shop is closed."

"How long is it going to be closed?"

"Until they can get the glass fixed."

"The glass that you broke?"

Ben would rather she didn't know about what happened last night, but he had a cut above his eyebrow that he couldn't explain away. So, he'd told her. And ever since then, she'd been elevating Kyla to princess status, and him to the Prince Charming who'd come to rescue her.

"Was Kyla very scared, Daddy?"

"Kyla was very strong. She called the police, and then she fought back. She's a very strong lady."

"I like her."

"I like her, too."

That was a little bit of an understatement. He was actually in love with her. He loved everything about her. He especially loved the way she made him feel— like he and his daughter were special to her. Like she might love them back.

It was too early to tell what would come of this new love, if anything at all. And that was okay. Right now, it was just enough to be feeling it again, to be feeling anything other than the bitterness that he'd grown so used to over the last few years. Kyla had come into his life, and lit it up. And he simply wanted to enjoy her warmth and light while it lasted.

He squeezed Gracie's hand. "Ready?"

"Affirmative. Daddy."

He reached up and knocked. And after a few seconds, Frances opened the door.

Smiling wide, she bent down and tweaked Gracie's nose. "What a surprise!"

Gracie laughed, delighted, as usual, with anything Frances did. "We brought worms."

"You brought worms? Well, you need to come in immediately, then. So we can share them."

"Is this a good time?" Ben asked. "We can come back…"

"Don't be silly. You're the best thing that's happened today."

Frances ushered them inside, fussing over Gracie's new dress.

"Is that new?"

"It's *brand*-new," Gracie said, giving her a little twirl. And then a curtsy, killing Ben dead.

"Isabel brought it over the other day," he said. "I think she likes it."

"It's absolutely adorable."

It was pretty cute. Yellow, with little honeybees all over it. Different than Gracie's usual palette of pink and purple, but it suited her. A ray of sunshine.

"Did I hear something about worms?"

This, from Kyla who was camped out on the sofa next to a crackling fire. She was leaning forward, trying to see into the entryway, a soft cream-colored blanket falling off one of her bare shoulders.

Ben's heartbeat slowed in his chest. She'd just grown more stunning since last night. Since the moment he realized how he truly felt about her. *Since the moment he'd nearly lost her.* She'd always been lovely. But he didn't think she'd ever be more lovely than she was right then, her dark hair wavy around her face, her gray eyes settling on him with a knowing look in them. He thought that look might be mirroring his own.

He leaned down close to Gracie. "Be careful around Kyla, okay?" he said into her ear. "I think she's a little sore, and her arm probably doesn't feel very good."

"Jacques is nursing her, Daddy," she whispered back. "Look. Right on her lap."

"He sure is."

Straightening up again, he nudged Gracie forward, and they headed into the living room. Jacques looked up and blinked at them through yellow eyes. He was taking his job very seriously, looking like he hadn't moved in hours.

Kyla beamed. She wore no makeup, and was so pretty that he almost forgot he was standing there holding flowers like a kid picking up his prom date.

"We brought you something to make you feel better," he said.

"Just you being here is enough to make me feel better." She winked at Gracie.

"Here," he said, handing her the flowers. And then the gummy worms. "Those are from Gracie."

"We had to go to the grocery store to get those, since Daddy broke your door."

Kyla laughed, glancing up at him. "He did break my door, didn't he?"

"And he got a cut on his eye."

Kyla frowned then, looking closer.

"It's nothing," he said.

"It bled a little," Gracie said. "But Aunt Isabel told him to put some medicine on it, and it'll be just fine. A-okay, that's what she said."

Frances poked her head out of the kitchen. "Gracie, I just took some peanut butter cookies out of the oven a few minutes ago. Do you want some with a glass of milk?"

Gracie's eyes lit up and she tugged on Ben's hand. "Can I?"

"Of course. Be sure and say thank you."

She ran into the kitchen, her sandals slapping on the hard wood floor.

After a few seconds, Kyla patted the spot next to her. "Come here, Ben."

He sat, careful not to jostle her.

"You do have a cut," she said. "Why didn't I see that before?"

"It's just a scratch. And you were a little busy with your own injuries."

"I'm okay."

But she wasn't. The bruises were clearly visible above the blanket, and he felt a slow fury build inside him. Gabe Mohatt was lucky he'd be safely behind bars for a while.

She reached for his hand, then brought it to her chest. The backs of his knuckles brushed against her breasts, and below his anger, there was a stirring of something else.

"I'm okay because of you," she said.

"If I hadn't gotten to you first, the sheriff's office would have. They were close, thank Jesus."

"I'm not talking about last night."

He watched her. Loving her. Seeing her then, in all her complexity and layers. How lovely they all were.

"You changed my life, Ben," she said quietly. "Thank you for following your heart that day."

And like she had so many times since coming home to Christmas Bay, she reminded him of that little girl she'd been. He'd had no idea all those years ago that Kyla Beckett would grow up so brave, so forgiving, so full of fire in her belly.

"I don't know that I could've done anything else," he said.

"I know. And I love you for it."

He looked down at her hand in his, and saw how perfectly they fit together. Like they were always meant to be. And maybe they were. Maybe the story he and Kyla had started so long ago wasn't done being told yet.

"Kyla," he began, not quite sure how he was going to say this. But knowing he needed to tell her what was in his heart. If he'd done the right thing in following it that day, he was going to follow it today. He owed that to himself. And he owed it to Gracie, too.

"Me first," she said.

He looked back up at her.

"I've been thinking. About leaving…"

He braced himself. But it didn't really matter what she was about to say. He still loved her. That wouldn't change. If she had to go, he'd just have to love her from afar.

"And I don't really want to," she said evenly, her eyes taking him in with that sexy, knowing warmth.

"Why is that?"

"Frances needs me. And you know, after everything that's happened, it just feels really good to be home. I've missed it here. I've missed the town, the people. The ocean… But there also happens to be this really great guy, and he's got this sweet little girl, and I've actually fallen for them both."

If he'd had any more doubts about letting himself fall for her too, they were gone in that instant. He reached out and cupped her cheek in his hand, reveling in the feel of her skin underneath his fingertips.

"You're too late," he said, with a slow smile. "I heard he's already kind of sweet on this lady from the candy shop. Maybe you know her…from up north somewhere?"

She smiled back as he leaned in close, his lips hovering over hers.

"No," she whispered. "She's from here. She's always been from right here."

Epilogue

Two months later...

Kyla pulled the box out of her car, tucked it under one arm and gazed across the lawn to the two-story brick building that sat overlooking the ocean. Welcome to Christmas Bay Middle School, the weathered sign out front read. Home of the Pirates—Arrgh, Mateys!

The chilly September wind blew Kyla's hair across her face, making it stick to her lip gloss. Brushing it back, she repositioned the box against her hip. It was heavy. She'd wanted to be prepared—her classroom was set up, but she'd saved her desk for last, a first-day-of-school tradition. Pictures, sticky notes, pens, a candy jar for her students (Frances had insisted on that part), and a brass apple paperweight that Ben had gotten her after she'd accepted the job.

With butterflies in her belly, she took a deep breath and headed up the walkway toward the concrete steps and the big familiar double doors. She was a seasoned teacher, but she had the same first-day jitters that she'd had when she was a student here herself. A full circle moment that made her heart squeeze. She had to keep reminding herself that she was no longer that awkward little girl with the glasses and broken spirit. She was grown now. She'd found safety again. She'd found happiness again.

Reaching for the door, she tightened her hold on the box, and hoped she wouldn't drop it on her foot. But the door opened before she could.

"Well, you're here early. Let me help with that!"

Her new principal stepped toward her and took the box. Masani Davis was tall, wore purple-framed glasses and a near-constant smile. Kyla had loved her instantly.

"Gracious, what do you have in here?" Masani asked.

"A few things for my desk. I might've gone a little overboard. I was excited."

"Not as excited as we are to have you," Masani said, holding the door open with her hip.

Kyla hurried through, thanking her and repositioning her canvas tote bag over her shoulder. She looked around. Not much had changed here since she was a kid—the same gleaming white floors, the spotless trophy case next to the front office and the perpetual smell of Tater Tots coming from the cafeteria, even though it was only seven thirty in the morning. The memories came rushing back, until she could almost hear her sixth-grade teacher reading aloud from *Where the Red Fern Grows*.

"Are you all settled into your new rental?" Masani asked as they made their way down the hall toward Kyla's classroom.

"Just about. I still have some boxes to unpack, but I wanted to finish painting first. I think I still have some in my hair. Caribbean Blue. It pops."

"And how's Frances doing? You said your sister is back helping her in the shop for the fall?"

Masani knew Frances from the booster club. And from bingo nights down at the community center. Kyla was beginning to realize that bingo was the social event of the week in Christmas Bay. She might have to drag Ben down there to see what all the fuss was about.

"She is. She loves it so far. Flexible hours and all the candy she can eat."

"Can't say I blame her there. Those sea salt caramels are to die for."

Kyla slowed, turning to the other woman, and feeling a sudden, genuine affection for her. She knew Masani was going to be a great boss. Maybe the best she'd ever had. "I just wanted to thank you again. For this job. For the opportunity. I know you had a lot of other applicants and I'm very grateful."

"Well, you were the best choice, by far. You're going to fit right in here, Kyla. We're all so happy you decided to stay in Christmas Bay." She came to a stop in front of Kyla's classroom door, where she set the box down. "And I happen to know of two other people who are happy, too."

Kyla raised her brows. "Who's that?"

"Why don't you go in and find out?"

Masani gave her a mischievous wink, and then walked away.

Kyla stared after her. Then turned to her door, which was open a crack. Tentatively, she gave it a push.

"Surprise!"

There, standing in front of her desk, were Ben and Gracie. Gracie was holding a caramel apple on wax paper.

She held it out to Kyla, grinning wide. Her permanent tooth was beginning to make its appearance in the gap that had stuck around for most of the summer. She wore a brand-new pink backpack, and baby-blue Converse All Stars. Just like the big kids, she'd announced, when Kyla and Ben had taken her to pick them out.

Ben stood beside his daughter, looking so handsome in his uniform that Kyla could only stare for a second. It was still hard to believe he was hers.

"You came to surprise me?" she finally managed.

"We wanted to wish you good luck on your first day," Ben said. "So we stopped on the way to drop Gracie off at school."

Kyla looked down at her. "Your first day of first grade! Are you excited?"

She nodded and bounced up and down on the toes of her new shoes. "Joe has Ms. Sims, and I have Ms. Bloom, but we'll get to see each other at recess and maybe at lunch, too."

"That's the coolest. I know you're going to have the *best* day."

"Can I FaceTime you when I get home?"

"We can do better than that," Kyla said, putting her hands on her hips. "Your dad and I thought we could all have pizza at my new place tonight. No furniture yet, but we can spread a blanket on the floor like a picnic. Would you like that?"

"Pepperoni?"

"Are gummy worms delicious?" She reached out and poked her belly.

"Yep!"

"Then, *yes*."

Ben tugged on a strand of Gracie's hair. "Why don't you go over and draw a picture of Jacques on Kyla's whiteboard?"

"So you can kiss her?"

Kyla's cheeks warmed. They'd been trying to move slowly for Gracie's sake. Taking the rest of the summer to ease her into the idea of her father dating again. But Gracie didn't miss a beat, and even though they tried to keep their hands off each other when she was close by, it was hard. It was like Kyla had been transported back to the best parts of high school. Sometimes making out with Ben was her favorite part of the day. Other times, just having his arms around her was.

Ben gave Gracie's bottom a pat. "Beat it, kid."

He didn't have to tell her twice. She loved drawing on the whiteboard.

"Don't forget to make him chunky," Kyla said.

"He's pleasantly *plump*," Gracie insisted in her best Frances voice.

Ben stepped close. "So," he said quietly. "Your first day. Are you ready? You look beautiful, by the way. If I'd had a teacher like you in the seventh grade, my heart would've been toast."

"I don't know about beautiful. But happy. Really, really happy."

He slid his arms around her waist. She felt his duty belt press into her hips, how his hand splayed warmly across the small of her back, making her feel safe.

She tilted her head back and surrendered herself to those feelings. All of them and more. What she'd really learned to do over the summer was surrender herself to love. To trust her heart to someone, fully, completely. And it was the most wonderful feeling of all.

"I'm happy, too," he said. "And I wasn't expecting that."

"Maybe we should just get used to expecting more. Maybe we deserve it."

He brushed her hair away from her face. "I love you, Kyla," he said simply. "I just do."

Smiling at that, she laid her head against his chest. And that love filled her to the brim.

* * * * *

Look for Marley's story,
Their All-Star Summer,
the next installment in the
Sisters of Christmas Bay miniseries
by Kaylie Newell.

On sale June 2023,
wherever Harlequin Special Edition
books and ebooks are sold.

#2959 FORTUNE'S DREAM HOUSE
The Fortunes of Texas: Hitting the Jackpot • by Nina Crespo

For Max Fortune Maloney to get his ranch bid accepted, he has to convince his agent, Eliza Henry, to pretend they're heading for the altar. Eliza needs the deal to advance her career, but she fears jeopardizing her reputation almost as much as she does failing for the sweet-talking cowboy.

#2960 SELLING SANDCASTLE
The McFaddens of Tinsley Cove • by Nancy Robards Thompson

Moving to North Carolina to be a part of a reality real estate show was never in newly divorced Cassie Houston's plans but she needs a fresh start. That fresh start was not going to include romance—still, the sparks flying between her and fellow costar Logan McFadden are impossible to deny. But they both have difficult pasts and sparks might not be enough.

#2961 THE COWBOY'S MISTAKEN IDENTITY
Dawson Family Ranch • by Melissa Senate

While looking for his father, rancher Chase Dawson finds an irate woman. *How could he abandon her and their son?* The problem is, Chase doesn't have a baby. But he does have a twin. Chase vows to right his brother's wrongs and be the man Hannah Calhoun and his nephew need. Can his love break through Hannah's guarded heart?

#2962 THE VALENTINE'S DO-OVER
by Michelle Lindo-Rice

When radio personalities Selena Cartwright and Trent Moon share why they've sworn off love and hate Valentine's Day, the gala celebrating singlehood is born! Planning the event has Trent and Selena seeing, and wanting, each other more than just professionally. As the gala approaches, can they overcome past heartache and possibly discover that Trent + Selena = True Love 4-Ever?

#2963 VALENTINES FOR THE RANCHER
Aspen Creek Bachelors • by Kathy Douglass

Jillian Adams expected Miles Montgomery to propose—she got a breakup speech instead! Now Jillian is back, and her ski resort hometown is heating up! Their kids become inseparable, making it impossible to avoid each other. So when the rancher asks Jillian for forgiveness and a Valentine's Day dance, can she trust him, and her heart, this time?

#2964 WHAT HAPPENS IN THE AIR
Love in the Valley • by Michele Dunaway

After Luke Thornton shattered her heart, Shelby Bien fled town to become a jet-setting photographer. Shelby's shocked to find that single dad Luke's back in New Charles. When they join forces to fly their families' hot-air balloon, it's Shelby's chance at a cover story. And, just maybe, a second chance for the former sweethearts' own story!

Get 4 FREE REWARDS!

We'll send you 2 FREE Books plus 2 FREE Mystery Gifts.

The Maverick's Marriage Pact — STELLA BAGWELL

Secret under the Stars — ELIZABETH BEVARLY

The Cowboy's Ranch Rescue — Lisa Childs

His Partnership Proposal

FREE Value Over $20

Both the **Harlequin® Special Edition** and **Harlequin® Heartwarming™** series feature compelling novels filled with stories of love and strength where the bonds of friendship, family and community unite.

YES! Please send me 2 FREE novels from the Harlequin Special Edition or Harlequin Heartwarming series and my 2 FREE gifts (gifts are worth about $10 retail). After receiving them, if I don't wish to receive any more books, I can return the shipping statement marked "cancel." If I don't cancel, I will receive 6 brand-new Harlequin Special Edition books every month and be billed just $5.49 each in the U.S. or $6.24 each in Canada, a savings of at least 12% off the cover price, or 4 brand-new Harlequin Heartwarming Larger-Print books every month and be billed just $6.24 each in the U.S. or $6.74 each in Canada, a savings of at least 19% off the cover price. It's quite a bargain! Shipping and handling is just 50¢ per book in the U.S. and $1.25 per book in Canada.* I understand that accepting the 2 free books and gifts places me under no obligation to buy anything. I can always return a shipment and cancel at any time by calling the number below. The free books and gifts are mine to keep no matter what I decide.

Choose one: ☐ **Harlequin Special Edition** ☐ **Harlequin Heartwarming**
                     (235/335 HDN GRJV)   **Larger-Print**
                                                  (161/361 HDN GRJV)

Name (please print)

Address   Apt. #

City   State/Province   Zip/Postal Code

Email: Please check this box ☐ if you would like to receive newsletters and promotional emails from Harlequin Enterprises ULC and its affiliates. You can unsubscribe anytime.

Mail to the **Harlequin Reader Service:**
IN U.S.A.: P.O. Box 1341, Buffalo, NY 14240-8531
IN CANADA: P.O. Box 603, Fort Erie, Ontario L2A 5X3

Want to try 2 free books from another series! Call 1-800-873-8635 or visit www.ReaderService.com.

HARLEQUIN
PLUS

Try the best multimedia subscription service for romance readers like you!

Read, Watch and Play.

Experience the easiest way to get the romance content you crave.

Start your **FREE TRIAL** at
www.harlequinplus.com/freetrial.